# Above the Pines

# Robert Bradford

A Thurston Howl Publications Book

ISBN 978-0-9908902-3-2

ABOVE THE PINES

Copyright © 2015 by Robert Bradford

First Edition, 2015. All rights reserved.

A Thurston Howl Publications Book
Published by Thurston Howl Publications
thurstonhowlpublications.com
Murfreesboro, TN

Mailing address:
4072 Hwy 200
Huron, TN 38345

jonathan.thurstonhowlpub@gmail.com

Cover design by Scott L. Ford

Edited by Angel Thurston; Proofread by Dustin C. Rogers

Printed in the United States of America
10 9 8 7 6 5 4 3 2 1

*To my parents, John and Jimmie Bradford, who always believed that I could climb my pine tree.*

*And to the victims of sexual and domestic abuse: This novel is a work of fiction, but sexual assault is not. I encourage all of you to seek the proper help and attention you need to successfully overcome the trauma. Make your voice heard. This novel is for you.*

# Skylines and Timberlines

*Above the pines*
*in the sky*
*above the beloved timberline*
*Hear the white heron cry.*

The poetry came to me in a fitful haunt. I'm reminded of words meant for peace—but only echo a hurt that never dies nor is forgotten. Though years have passed now, I still remember it all as if it were merely yesterday. I still remember the poem, the poet, and, of course, the pine.

\* \* \*

"I hate the woods," I said harshly as a branch snapped beneath my feet.

"Shut up, Sam," Isis said as she pushed through the woods, five feet in the lead and getting further away with every passing moment.

"Girls aren't made for this," I said, trying to dodge any branch that might snag my designer jeans.

"You're a disgrace to the gender," she said to me.

We were deep into an acre of wood that boarded our neighboring backyards. A three-mile walk took us to the center of the wood, away from our suburban neighborhood and away from everything it brought us. And most importantly to Isis, it brought us to her favorite pine. Her tree happened to be one of the largest, and unfortunately for me, the most climbable.

"I don't want to do this," I said as we approached the pine.

"Get over yourself," she said, grasping one of the branches and pulling herself upward. She didn't have to worry about her designer jeans—because she didn't wear any. She wore ripped, old, bleached shorts. It was her favorite thing to wear. Isis was a tomboy, if there was ever such a thing. I hesitated at first, but it was only a matter of time before she talked me into climbing the pine anyway. So I followed her. The sun was setting. The closer we got to the top, which was three broken nails and a scratch on my forearm later, we saw the orange sky. Clouds broke apart in the distance, like rising smoke. The sun fell below the skyline backdrop, shining off the metal buildings in a last ditch effort to bring about a twinkle of day. The orange lingered in the sky for a moment, like a warning before the stars interrupted.

Isis sat comfortably on a top branch of the tree. I sat, not so comfortably, a branch or two below.

"You've climbed this far ... might as well make the entire journey," Isis said.

I shook my head. "No. I'm fine."

"You can't always be afraid of heights, Sam."

"I climbed this much. Let that be enough."

Isis let out a small laugh and gazed off toward her left for what seemed like an hour. I only climbed high enough to peer over Isis. This was the only reason I ever joined her, the only reason I ever agreed to climb the stupid pine. Behind Isis, I could see the city—a beautiful skyline. It was the only place I wanted. I was fourteen-years-old, looking over my best friend toward the hopeful future. I imagined what city life would be like. I wondered what the people were like. I wondered what the food, the sounds, the music, the dancing was like. I lived so close, but I'd never been before. Isis didn't look toward the city—but to the mountains.

"Let's mountain climb soon, Sam," she said.

"Nope," I blurted out.

"Why not?"

"I don't want to."

"Have you ever mountain climbed before?"

"No."

"Then how do you know you don't want to?

"I don't like climbing things, Isis."

"You climbed this tree," Isis pointed out.

"But I didn't want to."

Isis giggled. The sun reflected off of her warm, tan skin. Isis, like her name, was beautiful. Green eyes that sparkled in the sun, and a body ahead of her age. All the guys wanted Isis. Nobody wanted me—and I couldn't really blame them. I had pale skin and flat blonde hair. I was thin—too thin. I didn't have curves like Isis, and I didn't have a chest like hers either. I was only a year younger than her, but Isis nearly had the body of an eighteen year old whereas I didn't even look my age.

"You'll get away from all this nature soon enough," she said, rocking back and forth on the branch.

"I hope so," I muttered.

"You will!"

"Don't jinx me."

"It's not a jinx. It's a fact. I dreamed about it." Isis said boldly, locking her eyes with mine. "I can see the future, remember?"

Isis meant it too. She believed she saw the future when she dreamed. Not every dream, but sometimes when she had a particularly realistic dream, she claimed they would eventually come to pass. I hardly believed her—but Isis stood by it. I never objected. She started believing in it around the time her mother died. She said that was the first dream that came true a week after she had it. She took it seriously and had ever since.

"What did your dream tell you about my future?" I asked, humoring her.

She smiled and looked toward the skyline. She knew I didn't actually believe her. "You make it to the city, and sooner than you think, too."

"Do you make it out to the wilderness?" I asked.

She frowned for a moment, and then smiled. "No. Not exactly. I go somewhere else."

"Where?"

"I don't know for sure, but it's nice."


We walked home that night, excited about our futures. I understood, even then, what the pines meant to Isis. There was something about being that high up that made you never want to come back down. There, according to Isis, we could escape from anything we wanted to. We had plenty we wanted to escape from. As we brushed past the twigs and leaves of the woods, my mind settled on what any thirteen-year-old girl might catch herself wondering about.

"Isis," I started, a little embarrassed, "what's it like to kiss a boy?"

"Not this again," she said, her tone exhausted.

"I'm just curious," I said.

"I've told you at least ten times before," she retorted. "Besides, it's not like I have a lot of experience myself."

"More than me," I muttered. At fourteen years old, I'd only had one boyfriend in my life, and that "relationship" didn't last long enough to warrant any kind of physical activity. Isis, on the other hand, who practically had boys fighting with each other over her, had her first kiss when she was twelve. She had so much attention from boys—one of the perks of developing before most of your peers.

"I've kissed two boys, Sam. Two. That's all," she said.

"I just want to be prepared!" I argued.

Isis laughed at me.

"Don't make fun," I said. I could feel my cheeks heating up.

"I'm not making fun, Sam. I'm just laughing at what you said. I was not prepared at all. I don't think you can be prepared for something like that ... it just happens. It's either good, or it's horrible," she explained.

"Was your first kiss good or horrible?" I asked.

Isis grimaced. "Awful, but I didn't know it yet. Not until I kissed Luke. That was a good kiss."

I sighed and smiled. "I can't wait."

"Easy there, tiger. Trust me, it's going to be awkward and bad at first, especially if you rush it. Don't rush it," she said.

"Calm down, Isis. It's not like I'm talking about having sex," I joked.

Isis scoffed. "Please don't even joke about that. If you think a first kiss would be awkward..."

I looked at her. She was shaking her head. "Isis ... you haven't ..."

Her arm flung across and pegged me in the shoulder. "Of course not!" she hissed.

"Okay! Okay!" I laughed, and so did Isis.

"You're so boy crazy now," she said, shaking her head.

"You're just crazy," I retorted. "I never wanna climb that tree again," I said. "It's too tall."

"You said that the last time," she said, smiling.

"I mean it this time."

"You said that the last time, too."

We reached the border—our wood had become our backyards once again. I hesitated as we parted ways, Isis to her house, me to mine. We lived in a humble neighborhood. It wasn't exactly trash, but it wasn't exactly something to be proud of either. You could definitely bet that every family on that block had some sort of struggle. Isis's was a tragedy.

I watched her back porch door slide open. DJ stepped outside, wearing a tank-top, self-inflicted ripped jeans, and a backwards baseball cap. DJ was the most beautiful boy I'd ever seen. Blue eyes, blonde hair, and teeth so white a girl couldn't stand it. It was unfortunate that he was Isis's older brother.

He smiled in our direction, although I know he was smiling at Isis. He loved his kid sister, and he hardly noticed me. DJ took his mother's death roughly, understandably, like Isis. It had been two years since their mother passed, and in that time, DJ had been kicked out of school and arrested three times—petty stuff. Nothing serious. He was an angry teenager who lost his mother. Isis brought out the best in him though. And for different reasons, he brought out the best in me. I waved. He waved back. If there was a person in the world shyer than myself, it was DJ.

"I'll see you tomorrow," Isis said with a grin. She giggled and ran toward the porch door. Isis's struggle was a tragedy. Her mother died, and her father spent so much of his time trying to provide for his children that he almost forgot he had them. At least she had her brother. I walked to my house. It wasn't any nicer than Isis's house. In fact, it was worse. And there wasn't an older, comforting brother waiting for me on the inside.

I usually always heard the television blaring from inside the house before I even opened the door. That night was no different. I heard whatever cheesy game show my parents were watching when I opened the door. My mother sat on a couch, with a cat and a pack of cigarettes in her lap, glaring at the television without blinking. My father sat across the room in an easy chair with a bottle of Jack Daniels laced between his fingers, snoring.

"Hey," I said as I passed through the living room. Neither one of them heard me—if they did, they didn't care.

My parents were alcoholics, and that is phrasing it nicely. They drank until they physically couldn't, and when they couldn't—they smoked. In elementary school, I was called Sam the Cigarette, because I always smelled of smoke. It wasn't until middle school, when I discovered perfume, that I started dousing myself in different scents in an attempt to mask the smell of tobacco that had survived the laundry. That's when I got a new affectionate nickname—Slut.

My room was very small, but it was my own. I shut the door behind me as soon as I entered, hoping that the wooden chunk would block out the noise of the game show blaring from the living room—it didn't. I didn't have much in that small room. I had old yellow wallpaper from whoever lived in the room before me, a twin bed, and a small wooden, carved-up desk that was my pride and joy. It was the one piece of furniture in the entire house that felt right. It was where I would sit and write—for hours. It was my only true passion in life, thus far. I wrote my way out of any situation I found myself in, as long as I could think of somewhere else to go.

I plopped on the bed and glared at the ceiling. I wrote about whatever came to my mind. I wrote about exciting adventures in the city. I wrote about getting away from this house, this neighborhood, and those pines. Sometimes, in these stories, I would be alone—traveling on my own to see the world far away from this dead end. Sometimes DJ would be there, and he would like me just as much as I liked him, but Isis was always in my adventures.

I debated for a long time if I would spend the night in my room or not. So many nights, I would sneak out, for one reason or another: my father was on a drunken binge, he and my mother were fighting, or they'd be openly having sex—either way they didn't care where I was or what I saw. So often, I would sneak out and walk across my backyard and into Isis's backyard. The back door didn't lock, and if I was quiet enough, I could slip in without her father, Jonathan, hearing me. Sometimes I would fantasize that I would pass Isis's room and walk down the hall to DJ's room. I never did of course. I would always crawl in bed with Isis, sleep until morning, and then leave before her father ever knew I was there. My father would never know if I were in my room or not. That's the great thing about having parents that don't care.

It's also the worst.

# The House Guest

I woke up the next morning in my bed, unable to make a decision before sleep overcame me. I was still wearing my tennis shoes. The alarm clock buzzed, faintly, somewhere in the catacombs of my room. Instead of trying to catch up, with a shower and some sort of excuse for breakfast, I opted to change clothes and walk over to Isis's house. We caught the bus to school every day together. Sometimes, when Jonathan didn't have to work, DJ would borrow the car and drive us to school, even though he was kicked out. I think he liked doing nice things for Isis, especially after their mother passed away. I loved those days the most. Any moments I could spend with DJ were moments I wanted. I rang the doorbell, and a moment later, Jonathan was inviting me inside.

"Get in here, Sam!" he said, as he ruffled the top of my head. I hated when he did that. He treated me like I was still six years old. He treated Isis that way, too, but he was always polite. He was a tall, lanky man, with jagged teeth that everyone saw when he smiled. Isis didn't look much like him—neither did DJ.

"Is Isis ready?" I asked.

"She should be soon, dear," he said.

He invited me into the house, and I followed. They had a small, three-bedroom house, with a tiny living room and kitchen tacked at the end. I'd spent just as much time there as I had my own home. It hadn't felt the same in quite some time though. Ever since Isis's mother died, the house lost something. It didn't smell the same anymore. It didn't feel the same. There weren't any freshly picked flowers in the window sills. Anna, Isis's mother, always had freshly picked flowers in their home. It was one of many things that made me jealous of Isis.

I waited for Isis. She didn't usually take long for school. I would wake up an hour early go shower, fix my hair, apply what cheap makeup I had, which usually always looked bad, and try to apply just the right amount of perfume. Isis could wake up, throw on an outfit, and look stunning compared to me. As I waited, I heard Jonathan's voice booming from the kitchen. He wasn't talking to me, and it didn't sound like he was speaking to Isis either. I felt my heart flutter when I thought about DJ. I imagined him sitting at the breakfast table, in one of his muscle shirts, and wearing a pair of sweatpants. He'd been drinking coffee and eating an egg and would occasionally smile, saying, "Hey, Sam."

I edged my way closer to the kitchen, in hopes of catching a glimpse of him. When I arrived at the edge of the kitchen, however, it wasn't DJ engulfed in a story with Jonathan, but an older man—not far from Jonathan's age. He was big and muscular, with a shaved head and a scar that stretched from the corner of his left eye to his ear. His arms were propped on the table, and I could see a tattoo that wrapped around his arm showing from under his short-sleeve t-shirt. The men laughed, and I could see the man's beady eyes glimmering under the light.

Jonathan noticed my presence and once again invited me in. "Don't be shy," he said.

I smiled, embarrassed to intrude in a conversation in which I didn't know half the party.

"Samantha, this is Sergeant Elliot Kerns. He's an old friend of mine from—wow, probably since we were you and Isis's age. Isn't that right, Elliot?" Jonathan said.

The stranger nodded as he sipped his coffee. He gulped and smiled intently at me. "Too many years ago," he said.

I smiled awkwardly. A chill ran up my spine the longer the man smiled at me. I couldn't figure out why.

"Mr. Kerns is going to be staying with us while he's in town for a couple of weeks. He's looking to buy a house nearby—finally retired from a life of protecting our country," Jonathan said proudly.

"You look too young to retire," I said, trying to be complimentary, but as soon as the words slipped my mouth, the smile faded from his.

"Well ... that's what happens when you take a few bullets to places like the knee. They either give you a boring office job or they let you go home. I decided to go home," Elliot said, sipping his coffee once again. "Great coffee, Jon."

"I'm sorry ..." I said, hesitantly.

"Its fine, honey," Jonathan said with a smile.

"Sam," a voice trailed behind me. I turned around to find Isis with backpack in tow, looking at me anxiously.

"Morning, honey," Jonathan said.

"Morning, Isis," Elliot mimicked.

"Morning. Ready to go?" Isis said to me.

"Sure."


"You know what today is," she said as she waited gleefully at the bus station.

"No?" I questioned. "It's ... Friday?"

"It's Friday, and Cory is back from the basketball tournament," she said. I saw a sparkle in her eye.

I rolled my eyes as I kicked a rock that poked beneath my shoe onto the street's asphalt. "You talk such a big game," I said, shaking my head.

"What is that supposed to mean?" she asked.

"You talk about Cory all the time, but you never do anything about it," I retorted.

"So?"

"So, why don't you do something about it?"

"I don't know."

"Because he's the boy?"

"No. That's not it, and you know it."

"Well, I can't figure out anything else, Isis."

She looked at me when I said her name. I could see the bus rolling down the street in the distance. I wanted to make my point before it arrived.

"Isis, you are the prettiest girl in the whole school. All the guys flirt with you. You could have any of them if you wanted, including Cory. Just do something about it already," I said.

"That's the pot calling the kettle black, don't you think?" she questioned, smirking.

I could feel my heart leap—I was terrified my expression gave myself away. "I don't understand what you mean," I lied.

"Really, Sam? Like there isn't a boy you think about—but won't say anything to?" she said.

It was as if DJ's name was written across my forehead. That is, if my flaming red cheeks hadn't burned the letters off yet. "There isn't anyone!" I lied again.

"Sam, be honest. I saw you talking to Steven Conners last week in gym," she said with a slight giggle. I could breathe again. "Steven? Are you kidding me?" I laughed. Isis couldn't be further from the truth.


"Students," Mr. Croft said, as he held a stack of papers in his hand. "I have your second exam graded. Some of you really improved … some of you didn't." He handed out the tests one by one to each student by placing them face-down on the student's desk. He started with my row. "If you're one of the ones with a satisfying grade, congratulations. If you're not— remember you can still turn in your extra credit assignment and it will really boost your grade. I promise," he went on.

He placed my test on my desk, and before he could move on to the next student, I flipped it over to study my grade. A 97. I was happy—it had improved a full letter grade. English was always my best subject. I loved literature and writing it.. Actually, I just really loved writing. I had a solid A in the class—but I did the extra credit homework anyway. The assignment was to write a poem about a place, person, or idea that meant a great deal to you. I adored that even in a literature class, Mr. Croft gave us a creative outlet.

As he moved to the next row, he laid Isis's test on her desk. She breathed heavily and turned it over. I could barely see the test, but I could tell by her reaction it wasn't good.

"Isis?" I whispered.

She didn't answer, or even look at me. Instead, she held up her exam for me to see. A 68. I grimaced.

"You can still bring up your grade," I whispered.

"How?" she snapped.

"The extra credit assignment," I replied.

Isis just rolled her eyes. A long-standing debate between the two of us, other than skyline verses timberline, was her ability to write. She didn't believe me when I told her she had a natural talent. I had read a few of her poems—but not many. Isis was private that way. Poetry was different for her. It was an intimate thing. It was beautiful —a thing of solidarity.

Cory reached up and tapped Isis on the shoulder. "How'd you do?"

"I did okay," Isis lied.

"I didn't," Cory replied, holding up his 77.

"You'll get 'em next time, tiger," Isis said, turning her attention forward.

Cory's eyes lit up and his cheeks flushed a little. It was obvious how much he liked Isis. He was a slave to her every word—her every movement. It was almost pathetic. Isis, though, had a better poker face at fourteen years old than most adults do. She let her lip curve up slightly, but only for a moment, knowing only I could see it. I didn't know why she played hard-to-get so much, but it worked for her. I've lost count how many poor saps have gone after her in the past year alone. I knew Cory was different, though. I knew Cory meant something to her, even if Cory didn't know it ... even if Isis didn't know it, either.

"I can't wait for high school next year," Isis said as we sat down in the cafeteria, both with a plate full of what were labeled as "steak nuggets." I couldn't agree with her more. We were on the verge of being freshman, and it wouldn't happen soon enough.

Another tray slammed down on the table across from us, startling me so badly I dropped a steak nugget onto the floor.

"Was that absolutely necessary?" Isis snapped at Guy Garrison who stood opposite the table from her, smiling slyly. Guy was about six foot one, which made him the tallest fourteen-year-old in the class. However, unfortunately for him, his height wasn't enough to mask his age—as his face was covered in red, puffy pimples.

"What gives, Isis?" he asked as he sat down at the table.

"Your pride, apparently," she retorted.

I laughed, and it caught Guy's attention. I couldn't help it. Isis was brilliant when it came to dry sarcasm. She was brilliant when it came to confrontation. Isis was brilliant at everything. There wasn't anything Isis was afraid of—not back then.

"What are you laughing at, Snow White?" Guy said to me.

It wasn't a compliment. My skin was so white it was almost sickening—especially sitting beside the tan beauty, Isis.

"Don't be a jerk," Isis said to him the moment I stopped laughing and looked down at my tray, uncomfortable.

"I'm just trying to talk to you," he pleaded with her.

I glanced up. He was glaring at her intently. She sighed with a smile and glanced around the room—letting him and everyone else know she was completely bored with what was happening.

"One date," he said.

"You've asked me out for one date every day this year—and

every day I've said no," she said.

"Come on, Isis. Who you holding out for?" he asked.

I wanted to blurt out Cory's name. I laughed to myself and suppressed the thought.

"Almost anyone else, Guy," she said.

"You know, if you don't want it, you shouldn't advertise so much for it," Guy said as he stood up, tray in tow, and walked away.

I felt an awful sinking feeling in my chest. I watched Isis's reaction, and I knew she felt the blow of Guy's remark. "I'm sorry, Isis. He is a jerk," I said.

She just shook her head. "Don't worry about it."

But she knew I would worry about it. I didn't have many friends — not like Isis, who'd befriended the entire school— save for Guy Garrison. Really, Isis was my only close friend and whenever she was verbally assaulted, especially for being overly developed for a barely fourteen-year-old, I would jump to her aid. Isis always stopped me though.

"It doesn't matter, Sam," she said as we walked back to class after lunch. "Guys like Guy don't bother me," she said, shrugging her shoulders.

"It bothers me," I repeated.

"Guy is just one of those popular jocks who is used to getting people's attention by being loud and overly aggressive. He's lame. I don't know why people pay attention to him," she said.

"Because, like you said, he's popular," I answered.

Isis waved her hand. "Popularity is a magic trick, Sam. It's fake," she said.

"You're one of the popular kids," I said, as we turned down another hall.

A few feet in front of us, standing by a locker, with a backpack flung over his shoulder, stood Cory. His black, wavy hair was messed up, and he was obviously sweaty—gym class, more than likely. He was deep in conversation with someone else until Isis passed and caught his eye. He did a double take, smiled, and waved. Isis lifted her hand, barely waving back, but smiling intently. She played it cooler than I could ever dream of playing it.

"Abra Kadabra," she said.


"I don't want to go back to the pines tonight," I complained, as we stepped off the bus and began walking towards our houses.

"We can't go anyway," she said.

"Oh, good," I said with a relief. "Why not?"

"I have to have dinner at home," she said, sulking.

"Why?"

"My dad's friend," she replied.

"Why is he here anyway? Your dad said he's moving here?" I asked.

"Something like that. I don't know. He's weird," she said.

Neither one of us said anything for most of the walk home, after that. I was about to tell her goodbye as we approached our front yards, when she blurted out, wrecking the silence.

"I had a bad dream last night," she said.

A bad dream was never a bad dream for Isis. If the dream was at all plausible, she feared it coming true; "the pitfall to having a superpower," she would say sometimes.

"What happened?" I asked.

She shook her head. "I don't know, but it's bad."

"It's just a dream," I protested, but she just looked at me with a disbelieving look, as if somehow I was the one who sounded ridiculous.

"You know that's not true," she said, as she started up her driveway.


I walked into the living room to find my parents in another world-famous screaming match. I couldn't understand either one of them well enough to deduce what was the cause of the night's argument, but I could almost guarantee it was about my mother's job or my father's drinking. My father was a construction worker for years before he injured his knee on the job so badly that he couldn't work anymore. He'd been drawing disability ever since, which resulted in him sitting in front of the television and drinking whatever piss-poor excuse for beer his government check allowed him to buy. My mother, on the other hand, held off drinking long enough to hold down a nine-to-five job, which barely paid enough to keep a roof over our heads. The only problem with that was it caused my father to be extremely jealous of all the male attention she received in the office.

I heated up a frozen T.V. dinner, which was what our refrigerator was always stocked with, and ate my dinner in silence and loneliness. My parents argued in the background, but I was plenty experienced at tuning them out.

By the time I finished eating, they'd each adjourned to separate ends of the small house. My dad, of course, remained in the living room with his precious television. My mother sat on the back porch, chain smoking a pack of Winston Lights. I debated going out on the porch to sit with her. I watched her as she crossed her legs and puffed a ring of smoke into the evening air. I saw a look of relaxation overcome her, but I knew it wasn't from the cigarette, not really. It was from the fact that she got away from my father for two minutes. I often wondered why she didn't leave him. I often wondered why he didn't leave her. I had to respect the loyalty they had despite the fact that they hated one another. That's the truth—they hated each other. Sometimes I felt like they hated me, too. Sometimes I felt like I hated them right back.


That night, as I changed into pajamas, I could hear them start fighting again. It was louder this time and more violent. My father's voice boomed from down the hall, and I could hear my mother's tears. I turned on my stereo and climbed into bed, hoping sleep would come soon and drown out the sounds of bitter people leading bitter lives. It was no use. My parents' vocal cords surpassed the volume setting of my CD player. I heard a loud and sudden crash against my closed door, followed by the sound of shattered glass. No doubt my father found enough rage to throw another beer bottle.

I thought about sneaking out of my bed and going to Isis's house—then I remembered their new house guest, the sergeant, and felt that maybe I should stay here. I couldn't intrude on her family all the time. Isis didn't have much—but she had a family that loved her. I thought about what it would be like to be a part of her family. I thought of DJ I would've loved so much to be in that house instead of my own.

I laid there for what felt like hours. I listened to the fighting. I thought about the city. I thought about the view that I could see from on top of Isis's favorite pine tree. I couldn't wait to be someplace like that—so far away from here.

I heard a sudden tap against my window, which hovered inches above my headboard. I jumped and felt goose bumps roll up my spine and down my arms. I peeked over the wooden frame, and there, huddled against my window with desperate green eyes, was Isis. I fumbled with the lock and slid open the window.

"What's going on?" I asked, my heart still beating rapidly.

"Can I stay with you?" she asked shakily. Her hair was tangled and drooped over her eyes.

"You know you can," I replied.

She crawled through the space and plopped down on my bed. She was under the covers with her back against me in seconds.

"What's wrong, Isis?" I asked, but she didn't answer.

I heard my parents yell once again. It sounded like they were in their bedroom now. I'd snuck away from them in the middle of the night to find solace with Isis for more nights than I could ever count—but Isis had never come here, looking for the same. I had no idea at the time why Isis needed me, my bed, and my house that night, but I knew that whatever it was, it must have been terrible.

# Sleepless Nights

I woke up the next morning expecting to see Isis fast asleep beside me. She was a heavy sleeper and when I spent the night with her, it was always me who was up with the sun. When I awoke, however, I found myself alone in bed. I contemplated the night before and expected, for some reason, to be able to deduce why Isis had crawled into my bed without hardly a word. She slept, curled up with her knees against her chest, in my bed—and I was clueless why.

I dressed for school and went by Isis's house, as if nothing peculiar had happened. I knocked on the door, and this time, to my pleasure, DJ answered the door.

"Hey, Sam," he said.

My lips parted and I forgot how to speak. I racked my brain for words but I didn't have any thoughts in my head except ones that I didn't want to say out loud. He hesitated and gave me an awkward smile. He wore athletic shorts and a tight t-shirt that read Boston Red Sox across his perfectly sculpted chest.

"Sam," I said, confused and dumbfounded.

He laughed, again, awkwardly. "Yeah...that's your name.

"Yeah. Sorry. Hey, DJ" I recovered, feeling completely

embarrassed. "Is Isis ready?"

He shook his head as he looked back toward the kitchen. "She's not feeling well today, Sam."

A horrible feeling hit the bottom of my chest. I wanted to ask him to check on her, or if I could check on her. I wanted to tell him about what happened the previous night, but couldn't have ratted her out like that...not when I spent so many nights climbing through her window.

"Oh. Okay. Tell her I said I hope she feels better," I said and walked away as fast as I could. I felt my cheeks burning from embarrassment. As I walked to the bus stop, I felt bad for being so short with DJ. Isis told me that since he dropped out of school after his mother died, he hadn't spent a lot of time with his friends. In fact, she said most of his friends stopped calling or coming around. When you become introverted, there aren't many other options. DJ hardly left the house. Unless it was to burn rubber in his dad's truck, and even to neighbors it was obvious he was in a hurry to get nowhere. Isis said even at home he wasn't truly there. I was never sure why. I didn't know the feeling of losing a mother. I barely knew the feeling of having one.

"Tell me about your week, Sam," Mrs. Oates said as I sat in the leather chair across from her big wooden desk.

She smiled at me, intently. The kind of smile you see politicians flash, with all their teeth, and bulging eyes. She was young—not a day over thirty. She was pretty, too, with long blonde hair and bright blue eyes with very light skin. It gave me hope that even pale people like me could turn out beautiful.

"Fine," I said, shortly. I didn't like visiting Mrs. Oates. She was a nice lady, but that was beside the point. When I was in seventh grade, a teacher noticed a bruise on my left arm. She asked me where it came from and I told her I fell down trying to climb a tree. When I came in with two or three more bruises, she asked me again. I told her I fell trying to climb a tree. That's when she asked me to stay after class one day, and tell her about how things were at home. I was honest with her. I was always honest about where I came from. I wasn't ashamed.

I didn't like it, but I wasn't going to lie about it, either.

"My father is a drunk and my mother is one step above that," I told her. My honesty got me into trouble. A police officer made a surprise visit to my house the next night. He gave my parents a hard time for drinking so much and doing it in front of me, but he found no other reason to remove me from the home. After he left, I received the biggest lecture I'd ever had from my parents. My father screamed so much I could feel his spit on my face. He was out of control, and he slapped me.

My mother screamed and picked me up off the floor. She turned on my father and began screaming at him instead. A few hours later he apologized to me. I nodded that it was okay but we've hardly spoken since then. From that day onward, I was required to spend one day a week during my gym period to come talk to the student counselor, Mrs. Oates.

And that's how I found myself sitting in her office, rocking from side to side, nervously, in the chair across her desk.

"What does 'fine' mean?" she asked, straightforward.

"It means fine," I replied.

We never talked too much. At least, I didn't. She would. Instead, I listened, nodded my head, made comments similar to hers, and reassured her my life was on track.

"How's your semester going?" she asked, examining my records. I always felt this was a redundant question. She had my grades right in front of her face. She knew what was going on.

"Fine," I said, steadfastly.

"Your English grades look fantastic," she said with pride.

"English is my favorite subject," I said.

She smiled and adjusted her small-framed glasses on her nose, peering back down at the piece of paper in her hand. Her smile faded.

"Bad week in Algebra?" she asked.

"Math is not my favorite subject," I replied.

"Neither is history, I take it," she retorted.

"History isn't anyone's favorite," I said.

She laughed. "Well, I can't argue with that, I'm afraid, but you need to bring these grades up, Sam," she said, earnestly.

"I can't do math," I repeated.

"You can and you will have to. You won't graduate high school with grades like this, let alone get into a good college," Mrs. Oates said.

"Maybe I don't want college. Maybe I don't need it," I replied. Although I'm not sure I actually felt that way, I was annoyed with Mrs. Oates's sense of entitlement, based on her higher education.

She almost scoffed at me, like I told a bad joke. "What do you want to do?" she asked.

I shrugged my shoulders. "I don't know."

"You don't know?" she said, unsatisfied.

"No."

"No idea?"

"None."

"That's hard to believe," she admitted.

"It's the truth."

She kept her eyes on me, closely, as if she was trying to read my mind. I felt awkward and uncomfortable, and looked down at my knees.

"What do you like to do, Sam?" she asked.

I shrugged again.

"Be honest."

I hesitated and glared at the clock. I had another thirty minutes with her. Thirty minutes that would go by a lot slower if I continued being so resistant.

"I like to write," I admitted.

At these words, Mrs. Oates's eyes lit up. She smiled and sat up straight, looking shocked and impressed. I hated that she looked shocked.

"You're a writer?" she asked.

"I don't think I'd call myself a writer," I replied.

"What do you like to write?" she asked, ignoring my statement.

"Anything. Poems. Plays. Short stories. They're not very good, though" I admitted.

"I'm sure they are," Mrs. Oates replied.

It was a cheesy reply. She hadn't the first clue if I was a good writer. She just wanted to fuel my fire—and I guess I couldn't blame her for that, after all, that was her job.

"Do you let anyone read these works of yours?" she asked, eagerly.

"Sometimes," I said.

"Your parents?"

"Good gosh no," I snapped.

"Your friends?"

"Isis."

"Isis Cassidy?"

"That's her."

Mrs. Oates nodded her head slowly. "She's a good friend of yours, isn't she?"

"The best," I replied.

Mrs. Oates took off her glasses and laid them on the desk. "How are things at home, Sam?"

"They're fine," I stated.

"You'd tell me if they weren't, right?" Mrs. Oates asked.

"Yes," I lied.

"Good. I don't want you to ever be scared to tell the truth," she said.

"I'm not," I replied, quickly.

Mrs. Oates peered at me for a moment. She was known as the human lie detector. I dared to lie, on a weekly basis—but she never caught me. Some lie detector.

"I think you should focus on your writing, Sam," she started. "I think it'd do you some good. And besides, you never know, it could turn into a career one day," she smiled.

"Maybe," I shrugged.

"I'd love to read something you wrote, one day, if you feel like sharing."

I know she meant well. I knew that then, but I couldn't bring myself to trust her. That was my thing. If Isis really had a superpower, if she really could see the future, then my superpower was that I knew the people you could trust....and the ones you couldn't.

That night I laid in bed, listening to my mother cry, in her drunken rage, while my dad snored in his easy chair. I had no idea what she was crying about, but I'm sure it was something that my father did do, didn't do, or didn't do right. I would've given anything to crawl out my window and into Isis's, but when I stopped by after school, her father, Jonathan, said she were still feeling ill. Just as I was drifting off to sleep, to the sound of my mother crying, I heard an alarming peck on my window. I jumped but calmed down when I saw Isis. I opened the window and shook my head.

"You gotta stop scaring me like that," I sighed.

"Can I sleep over?" she asked quickly.

She was wearing an oversized t-shirt that drooped down to her knees. Her hair was ruffled, and her nose was red. Her eyes were bloodshot—she'd obviously been crying.

"Yeah," I said, changing my tone and helping her over the headboard. "What's wrong?"

Isis shook her head.

"Tell me," I demanded.

Isis just shook her head again and laid on the bed. "I don't want to talk about it."

I lay down beside her, and she once again turned her back to me and curled up into a ball.

"I wish you would talk to me, Isis," I said.

She didn't reply. She never did. I hardly slept at all that night, and I know for a fact she didn't either. We just lay there in silence. Occasionally, I would hear Isis sniff, or whimper. Every time I heard her, it felt like a knife stabbing through my heart. I had an awful feeling about my best friend and I couldn't even talk to her about it. It was a sleepless night for us both. I don't think Isis wanted to sleep. I don't think she wanted to dream—in case she saw the future.

# Changeling

The rest of the week had been almost identical to that first sleepless night. Isis returned to school, but she was quiet. She told me she still wasn't feeling too well, and that the only reason she returned to school was because she had to or else she'd fall too far behind. She barely spoke unless I asked her a direct question and even then she kept her answers short and to the point. My concern for her was growing stronger with each passing day.

On Saturday, like most Saturdays, I couldn't stand being at home any longer than I had to, so I ventured over to Isis's house. I felt awkward, because of how distant she'd been to me all week, but I took my chances. I rang the doorbell, but no one answered. I waited, and knocked on the door but still no one came. I finally walked around the house to the backyard, hoping to catch a glimpse through the screen door that led to their porch. I realized how annoying I must've been, but I knew that if Isis was home and feeling like her old self again, she'd want to see me.

When I walked around, however, I was caught off guard by the sight of DJ, who was by the shed, shirtless, with his head under the hood of a Chevy Nova. It was a beautiful fixer-upper. Blue and purple paint, with bald tires. The car didn't have my attention, though. I glared at him for too long. I'd never see him shirtless before. It was fantastic. Before I could cut away, he raised his head up and caught eye contact with me. He smiled.

"Hey, Sam," he said.

I waved awkwardly and walked toward him.

"What are you doing?" he asked, as he picked up a bottle of water and sucked half of the contents down his throat.

"I...I was looking for Isis. Is she feeling better?" I asked.

DJ shrugged his shoulders. "I think so. Actually, she's not here right now."

"Oh," I said, disappointed. "Well...I'll see ya later," I said, as I began to make my way back to the house.

"Hey, Sam," he said.

I turned around, quickly. My heart was pounding. He looked at me for a long moment before he spoke, almost as if he was studying me, but I chalked it up to wishful thinking.

"You can stick around for a little while. I think she'll be back soon. She went with dad to run some errands," DJ said, picking up a towel and wiping his hands.

"Okay," I said, a little too eagerly. I propped myself up on a stack of tires beside the car. "Where did they go? Isis hates doing errands with her dad," I said, bluntly.

DJ laughed. "Yeah, Dad is slow, but I think she was just looking to get out of the house for a few minutes."

"How long have you had the car?" I asked, changing the subject.

"I bought it last week. I've been saving up for a long time. It obviously needs some work, but I'm doing it all myself," he said, proudly.

"That's impressive," I said, giddily.

He smiled. "Thanks."

"DJ" a voice yelled, nearly startling me off of the stack of tires. I looked toward the porch, where I heard the voice. Jonathan's friend, Elliot stood at the screen door. He looked bigger than I remembered. "Finish up with the car and come find me in the kitchen," Elliot barked.

"Why?" DJ protested.

"Because your father wants us to unclog the pipes. Now, get moving," Elliot said, forcefully. He glared at me for a moment and I felt a chill go up my spine. However, he turned back toward the house and entered without saying another word.

"Whatever," DJ muttered under his breath.

I watched him gather his tools together. His muscles flexed as he stacked them into his tool box.

"What's his deal?" I asked, picking up on the vibe that DJ didn't care for their houseguest.

"He's a jerk," DJ stressed. "He's more than a jerk. He's kind of a creep. And he's so bossy. He's been bossing me around all week—ever since he got here. He came down here and tried to tell me how to take out the transmission. Can you believe that? Trying to tell me what to do to my car and how to do it," DJ said.

"Maybe he was just trying to help?" I questioned.

DJ shook his head. "No, he was just being a controlling know-it-all."

"What did you mean by creep?" I asked.

"He just…glares at me. He watches every move I take. Not just me, he watches Isis, too. He's just a creepy dude," DJ explained

A nervous feeling twisted in the pit of my stomach.

"I can't wait for him to leave," DJ said.

"When is that?" I asked, eagerly.

"I don't know. It's not soon enough, though. It's really not soon enough."

"I think I want to do him," Isis's words were jagged and unforgiving.

"What?" I asked, perplexed. We were facing the school's common area. Our friends and foes gathered there every morning and every afternoon, including Cory. It had been a week since Isis had started coming back to school, but it was becoming increasingly obvious that she came back different. She gifted her beautiful green eyes into my direction and smiled a guilty-as-sin smile.

"You heard me, Sam," she teased.

I shook my head. Part of me was proud that Isis had the bravery to bluntly say, as she glared at Cory across the commons, that she wanted to have sex with him. Isis, however, had always been one to heed the risks of sex. It was an impressive trait of hers. After all, she was probably the most desired teenage girl in our entire school—yet she was the one girl that would say no faster than you could ask the question.

"Are you two even…dating?" I asked, knowing how cheesy the question sounded, and knowing without a doubt that the answer was no.

She shrugged her shoulders. "We could be." And that was all Isis said about the subject, or on any subject, throughout the rest of the school day. It wasn't until later, when school was over that she found room to include me in conversation once more.

"What are we doing after school?" she asked, eagerly.

"Going home?" I questioned, confused, as this was our normal routine.

Isis simply shook her head. "Not today. We always go home. We're not going home today."

I had to admit I didn't mind the idea of skipping our bus to Park Street, and instead finding a wild adventure, or even a tame adventure, to indulge ourselves in for a Friday afternoon, but Isis's newfound personality traits, admittedly, concerned me.

"What did you have in mind? A grand adventure?" I asked, still subconsciously walking toward our bus, just outside the school doors.

She grasped me by the arm and pulled me toward her. "Something like that…and I don't know where you think you're going, but we're not getting on that bus," she scoffed.

It wasn't until that moment when I saw the look, almost a sparkle, in her eye, and a twitch of a manipulative smile arise on her face that I realized she had a plan the entire time to stop us from going home that Friday afternoon.

"Yes," she started, as if I was the one with an idea. "We'll have a grand adventure. Not an adventure…but The

Adventure."

"The Adventure," I mocked, in the same tone.

"Yes, The Adventure. We're going on the adventure, Sam," she said with a giggle.

I laughed out of nervousness. I was nervous. It was like one of those moments when you flip through a photo album, and find an old picture of yourself. You stare into your own eyes, and you scarcely recognize the person in your clothes—in your skin. I stared at Isis. I saw her pretty hair, her gorgeous eyes, her familiar smile, and her same, solemn, smooth voice…and had no idea who was in front of me.

Later that same night, after Isis had spent most of the afternoon in ambiguous planning, we met Carly in the Shop-and-Save parking lot, a grocery store on the very edge of town. Carly walked out of the Shop-and-Save, in a tight pink tank top and white shorts, carrying three bags in her hands. She was obviously older than both Isis and myself, no younger than twenty-one, I suspected, considering a case of beer could clearly be seen through one of the white plastic bags she grasped. My heart felt like it skipped a beat as I was still clueless to what the night had in store.

"Hey, whore," Carly said, laughing.

"Hey," Isis said, hesitantly.

"Relax, you're not getting caught," Carly replied.

Isis just shook her head. "It's not that. Uh, Carly—this is Sam," she said, motioning half-heartedly toward my direction.

Carly glanced at me and smiled. She had short, brown hair with cheap-looking highlights on the tips of the curls. I smiled, but only briefly and barely. I'd never heard Isis mention an older friend named Carly before.

"Carly dates my cousin Lee," Isis explained. "And she's also a college student old enough to buy us beer."

Carly hit Isis, playfully, but firmly, on the arm. "Lower your voice, child."

"Sorry," Isis replied.

I tried to keep my face expressionless, but of course, that was impossible. I was perplexed at the conversation happening.

"Carly's parents are out of town for two weeks!" Isis's eyes sparkled in that unpleasant way once again. "And we're going to have a party."

Carly preceded to load the cases of alcohol into the back of her jeep. "Come on, girls, we don't want to be late to our own party."

My stomach twisted and turned, as Carly's jeep twisted up a curvy, gravel driveway, which led to a large, blue house on a hill. I contemplated what was happening, and still found myself astonished that Isis was so on board with this level of deception. Despite the issues we had with our home lives and our families, Isis was always very close to her father and brother. It was one thing for me to lie and sneak out of the house—considering my parents were never sober long enough to notice--but it was completely different for Isis.

In fact, it was completely out of character for Isis to even attempt a party like this one. Isis always preferred to be in a tree somewhere, not in a stranger's house with a bottle of liquor.

Carly parked and hopped out quickly to greet Sam's cousin, and another female who stood on the back porch smoking cigarettes. I used the opportunity to pull Isis a couple of steps away.

"What is going on?" I asked, hesitantly.

"A party," she shrugged.

I shook my head. "No, I mean really."

She sighed, as if I were the one who was insisting upon something against our standard social interactions.

"What's your deal?" I asked her.

She watched me, perplexed, before she responded. "What do you mean?"

"Suddenly we're the type of people that drink and go to parties?"

"We're not kids anymore, Sam, we're growing up. Things change."

"Like this, though? Isis what is going on? What's—"

"Look, Sam. I thought we'd have some fun for once in this stupid town. I thought we'd try to see what it was like to be a little grown up. I thought it would be nice to spend a night not dreaming of where we will be one day but be somewhere for once. I just wanted out of the house for one night. Actually, for two weeks' worth of nights because Carly said I could stay here with her," Isis snapped.

"Do you really think that's a good idea?" I retorted.

"Sam…you just don't get it," she replied.

"Then explain it to me. Explain why you've gone from crying in my bed every night to acting like a completely different person? What's going on with you?" I stressed.

"It's just alcohol!"

"That's exactly what my parents say!" My voice squeaked, as if it broke. As if I broke it trying to choke out the truth.

Isis stopped. Her frown disappeared and her eyes seemed to shrink. I could feel the tears rising in mine. I could see it rising in hers, too. There were no more screams, only whispers.

"I'm sorry," Isis said, as she wrapped her arms around my neck.

"Me too."

"I don't want to go home tonight, but if you do, I can have Carly take you," she said.

I was hurt and somewhat appalled that she still wanted to stay. We always told each other we wouldn't turn out like our parents. Why would that night be any different?

"It's not going to get crazy. It's just a few people—just drinking. Nothing crazy," she said, more concerned about my response now than before. "I'll stick by you."

I nodded. She smiled briefly and turned toward the house, motioning me to follow her. I followed, sheepishly, as I always did when it came to Isis. I followed her to that big blue house, as if it were those pines. I knew I'd follow her as she climbed while I hope and pray that we both didn't fall.

It became obvious to me, though, as the night progressed, that we weren't in those pines. We weren't anywhere near them. We were in a house filled with people—most of them considerably older than us. There were a few classmates, familiar faces, but that was it. Not faces I wanted to see—faces

Isis and I always avoided. After an hour of socializing and holding a beer without sipping it, I stepped out onto the patio, which connected to a swimming pool. The night was cool and there wasn't a cloud in the sky. I glared up at the full moon as it loomed over us. Music blared from the living room and people laughed and yelled, no doubt a direct result from their intoxication. Isis didn't seem to be drunk, but she seemed to be just as heavily influenced as the rest of them. Cory had been invited to the party, on par with her request, and the two of them had spent the entire night flirting with each other.

I wanted to see the two of them together; they had both pined over each other for what felt like months, but something about this setting felt off—it felt wrong. I sighed and tossed my cheap beer onto the grassy area beneath the patio and left the red cup alone on the rail. I thought, in a moment of personal doubt, that perhaps I was being too hard on Isis and the situation. After all—if Isis was in a time of self-discovery; who was I to stand against her? It made me realize my own personal bias against alcohol—it took my parents away from me and I feared it would do the same to my best friend. That wasn't something I would ever be prepared for, no matter what the cause.

I thought of DJ and smiled. I was never sure what it was about him that made me smile at the most random of moments. I kicked my shoes off, moved to the edge of the pool and sat down, letting my feet dip into the cold water. I imagined DJ sitting there with me, or maybe even swimming with me—shirtless. I thought about us watching the moon and the stars together. I wondered if that was even something DJ would want to do…or would he rather enjoy a beer too, or do cannonballs into the deep end? Any of it would be fine, as long as I spent that time with him.

"Is this seat taken?" a deep voice, from behind, startled me. I looked up to see a tall boy, with blonde hair and two beers in his hands, looking down at me with a smile.

"Uh," I muttered.

He plopped down beside me. "I'll take that as a no," he said, and handed me one of the beers. I awkwardly, as always, took the bottle.

"You didn't have to—"

"It's not like I bought it or anything," he said with a laugh.

I forced out a laugh.

"I'm Colin, by the way," he said.

"Sam," I replied.

"I haven't see you around here before—are you a friend of Carly's?"

"I'm Isis's friend. You know, Carly's cousin."

"Oh, that explains it. Do you not like beer?" he asked, as he eyed my untouched bottle that I had carefully placed beside me.

"I...don't really drink. I'm sorry."

"Don't apologize to me. I'm sorry. I just assumed, since you're here."

"Well I kinda got...roped into coming."

"Playing your best friend's wingman. Making sure she's safe. Making sure she doesn't do anything dumb, right?" he said.

I nodded and looked back toward the house. I could see the living room from where I was sitting, through the glass of the French doors that led out to the patio. I saw several people laughing, talking, dancing, and drinking. And, I saw Isis, sitting in a corner, talking to Cory.

"Something like that, yeah, I guess."

"Well she's talking to Cory. Cory is a solid guy."

"You know Cory?"

"Best friends since the first grade."

"You're our age?"

"I'm sixteen and I go to a private school, but I've lived beside him my entire life."

I nodded and looked back down at the pool water. The night was so dark, save for the bright moon over our heads, which reflected off the seemingly black liquid that rippled around my ankles. "

"Same story with Isis and me," I said.

"Well she's good to have a friend like you," he said.

I scoffed and looked at him. "On what grounds? You don't

even know me."

"You're right—I don't. I was banking that you'd just take the compliment and leave it alone," he said and we both laughed. Maybe I was being too paranoid about the party—maybe we were seeking a great adventure. It might not be the adventure but, perhaps it was a start to one. That's really what I thought at that moment, back then, ankle deep in cold water, forgetting for a moment about the rough few weeks we'd been through.

"Sammy!" I heard an obnoxious voice call from the French doors. Guy Garrison approached, cheesy smile and all, with a red solo cup clinched in one hand—not to mention the smell of vodka and soda on his breathe.

"Well, what do we have here—Colin? You're putting the moves on Sam?" Guy said, chuckling a little bit as he walked around the edge of the pool.

I blushed and looked down at my feet, making circles beneath the water.

"It's not like that, Guy," Colin explained.

"Ouch, burn again, right, Sam?" Guy said.

"You think you've had too much, Guy?" Colin coolly said.

"Don't be such a wimp, Colin. Are you gonna give it to Sam or not?"

"Guy. That's enough," Colin said, stronger this time.

Guy waved his arm dramatically as he plopped down in a lawn chair near the pool's diving board.

"Calm down. It was just a question," Guy said, shrugging his shoulders.

A silence arose, and I just tried to play off the entire incident with a laugh and a rolling-of-the-eyes. A few moments passed and I had contemplated pulling my feet out of the pool, finding my shoes and going inside to check on Isis. Just as I was working up the nerve to tell Colin goodbye, however, hoping that Guy wouldn't make any comments, the jerk in the lawn chair beat me to it.

"I mean, Sam is a little plain, Colin. But I bet she's good," Guy said, taking a sip from his cup.

"That's completely inappropriate," Colin retorted.

"She doesn't look as good as the other one—Isis. Not as curvy or as…gifted if you know what I mean. But still—I bet she'd really put her one hundred percent into it.

My face felt like it was on fire. I don't know what was bothering me more—the embarrassment or the rage. "I wouldn't give you my one hundred percent," I snapped.

Colin laughed, heartedly. Guy lost his smile. He didn't say anything, but a few seconds later, he got up from his lawn chair and walked over to Colin and myself. I felt strangely uncomfortable, but did everything I could to ignore him. He stood on the other side of me and glared downward. "At least I could show you what you've been missing out on," he said.

I didn't pay attention to him. I looked to Colin instead, but even he couldn't help but feel stressed by the bully standing just a foot away from me.

"It's not like you got a lot of room to be picky. You're decent-looking when you're sitting by yourself out here—"

"She's not alone," Colin said.

I had enough with the situation and I stood up, yanking my feet out of the pool. "I've had quite enough of your testosterone for one night, Guy. Thanks," I said and started to walk toward the patio when he grabbed my arm and pulled me close to him.

"Listen, did you come here to whore yourself like your friend or did you come here to be a prude?" Guy said, and with that, he grabbed my wrist and brought it towards his belt.

I groaned and tried to pull my arm away but I couldn't break Guy's hold—however I didn't have to—thanks to Colin.

Colin stepped up, and without saying a word shoved Guy to the ground, and pulled me back with his other arm before I fell, too.

Guy grimaced as he situated himself off the ground, and before either of us could do or say anything, he charged at Colin pulling back to punch him in the face, which inadvertently knocked me in the jaw and sent me spiraling into the cold pool.

It was several seconds before I could find my way to the surface, and when I did, I gasped and coughed for air.

"Sam!" I heard a voice. I struggled to dog paddle to the closest side that I could find, while attempting to wipe the water from my eyes

"Sam! Are you alright?" another voice called. I clinched the side and instantly felt embarrassed. A few partiers paused momentarily to join the patio in order to find out what was happening. Mortified, I lifted myself up and out of the water. Colin darted over to me.

"Are you okay?" he asked. "Oh my gosh, you're bleeding!"

I felt my nose and he was right—blood dripped onto my fingertips. "Great," I said.

At that moment, the music ceased. Carly reached the patio.

"What's going on out here?" she said, her voice stern.

The crowd, including Carly, looked to me. "I...I.." I stuttered, perplexed as to what to say.

"We were all talking and she tripped. She busted her nose on the side of the pool and fell in," Guy said.

I glared at him for having the audacity to say such a blatant lie after what he pulled.

"That's not what happened," I scoffed. "Is it, Colin?"

Colin stayed silent. I looked toward him. He seemed uncomfortable—overwhelmed.

"Colin?" I repeated.

"Yeah, Colin, what did happen?" Guy said, a small smirk arising on his face.

"Guy and I were playing around...Sam tried to get out of the way and she tripped and fell in the pool, like Guy said," Colin lied, sheepishly. He looked toward Guy and Carly, refusing to make eye contact with me. It was in that moment that I realized what exactly Colin was in life—he wasn't a DJ but he wasn't a Guy either. He was something different and worse in some ways. He was a coward.

I brushed past him and the rest of the poolside crowd to reach Carly.

"I need to use your phone," I demanded.

"There's one in the kitchen, sweetie. But hey, you're not calling any parents, are you? We could all get in a lot of trouble here if anyone found out about this—even you," she said.

I was furious at her implications—not to mention her priorities.

"I'm not—I'm just calling for a ride," she said.

"One of us can take you home, sweetie," she said.

"Honestly, I don't trust anyone here," I said, as I moved into the kitchen.

"I'm sorry you slipped, sweetheart but you don't have to leave; I can clean up your nose. You gotta be careful, though, because it's slippery out there," Carly said.

"I DIDN'T SLIP," I yelled. "Now where's the phone? I'm calling for a ride and I need to find—" I stopped. I glanced around the living room. A few straggler party goers, who either didn't care about the commotion outside, or were too drunk to know there was any, remained, watching the confrontation between Carly and myself. There was no Isis, however, and there was no Cory.

"Where's Isis?" I asked, hesitantly.

Carly glanced around. "I don't know," she said, shrugging. Maybe she's upstairs."

"Why would she be upstairs?" I asked, knowing the obvious answer.

Carly laughed and rolled her eyes. "I mean, she is maturing, Sam. Her and Cory hit it off pretty well," she said, turned on her heel, and walked back toward the living room.

I walked up the stairs, unsure of exactly what I was going to do…but it had to be something. At the top of the stairs, I could easily see three bedrooms, but only one had a closed door. I slowly approached on tip-toes, hoping that between the top stair and the door knob, I might concoct some plan that would enable me to get Isis out of there before anything happened that she would regret. I waited patiently by the door, waiting for inspiration to strike. Nothing happened. I contemplated walking away—it wasn't my business after all, but just before I turned around and descended the stairs, I heard a muffled scream and a shattering of glass.

I didn't hesitate. I rushed the door and forced it open as quickly as I could. I found Isis standing in the corner of the room with a broken lamp by her feet. Cory sat on his knees, on the bed. His shirt tossed to the floor. He watched me, then Isis, confused and bewildered. Isis was clothed, but it was obvious, by her hair and the wrinkles of her shirt, where the moment was taking them.

"Sam," Isis said.

"Are you okay? I heard you scream!" I said.

"I'm...fine. Just go," she said.

I shook my head. "You screamed and broke a lamp."

"Just go, Sam," she said again.

"Isis, if you want to leave," Cory started.

"No," she snapped.

But her body said yes. She huddled in the corner and crossed her arms. She was uncomfortable to every degree.

"I do," I said.

"What?" she asked.

"I want to go," I repeated.

"Sam..." she started.

"No. I want to go. I want to go now. This is insane," I said, harshly.

"I can take you guys home," Cory said, assuredly, as he reached for his shirt.

"It's okay...I called someone," I stated.

"Who?" Isis asked, casting a look at me.

"DJ," I said.

Her eyes widened and she gritted her teeth. "Sam!"

'What?"

"I told you I wanted to say here for a couple of weeks! With Carly! If DJ sees this party, he'll tell Dad. And Dad will never let me come back!"

"Oh, yeah, that sounds like a horrible thing!" I mocked.

"Screw you, Sam! You've ruined everything!"

"Do you notice that I'm dripping wet from head to toe?" I barked. "Because I got pushed into the pool. I'm guessing you didn't notice my busted nose, either. That's thanks to Guy Garrison, who hit me and knocked me into the pool as he attempted to attack a guy who was sticking up for me, after he made a pass at me," I stated.

Isis's expression softened. "He what?"

"He tried to force himself on me, Isis. Because of this stupid party. I want to leave. You can stay. I didn't even tell DJ you were here. He doesn't have to know. Just stay here, but I'm leaving," I said.

Isis looked down for a moment. She eyed Cory on the bed and then back at me. "He really tried something on you?" she questioned.

I nodded and as soon as I did, Isis stormed out the door and rushed down the stairs. I followed and called after her. She didn't stop. She wouldn't stop. She thrust opened the French doors and found Guy talking to another girl near the pool. I stopped by the doors, too cowardly to do anything else.

"Hello, Isis," Guy said as she saw her approaching him rapidly. "What brings you out—"

Isis slammed the palms of her hands into his chest and watched as Guy fell off balanced, and landed into the pool. A few of the others laughed. A few of them even cheered. I darted outside and grabbed Isis's arm.

"You didn't have to do that!" I said.

Isis looked at me with a cold stare—as if she was about to throw me into the pool as well. "Never let something like this happen again," she barked.

"Isis I couldn't—"

"Next time call me. Call someone. Call me. Make sure I'm there. Don't call DJ or anyone else. You come find me. You should've found me tonight, not DJ, me. Do you understand? She snapped.

"Yes," I said, shamefully.

At that moment, I saw headlights make their way up the darkened driveway and before either of us could say anything, I saw Jonathan's pickup truck awaiting in the driveway, with DJ in the driver's seat.

A few of the others went inside trying to avoid being seen by the big brother who just crashed the party. Isis stormed off in the direction of the truck and I followed suit. She opened the passenger door and slid into the middle and I sat beside her.

"What's going on, Isis?" DJ asked, displeased.

"Just don't say anything," she said.

DJ eyed me as I shut the door. "Are you okay, Sam? You're soaking wet."

"I'm fine," I said with the smallest voice I could find.

DJ drove away, without another word. Isis didn't say anything to either one of us the entire trip. In fact, she hardly budged. She glared out the windshield…as if she was looking at something intently. I could only see a dark road with the occasional street light. Isis saw something else and, whatever it was, I was almost positive I didn't want to see it for myself.

When we arrived home and stepped out of the truck, I was prepared to apologize to Isis for calling her brother and ratting her out, but before I could do so Isis stormed inside without a word.

"Don't worry," DJ said, noticing my expression. "She'll be okay."

I smiled, weakly. Despite my concern about Isis, any moment DJ and I had together, I dreamt of it being a positive one.

"You're a good friend to her," he said. "You take care of her. That's a very admirable quality," he said, gazing at me.

I couldn't decide how to act. As pleased as I was that DJ was looking at me so admirably was flattering—but the night's events with Isis casted a heavy cloud over me.

"She takes care of me, too," I said and turned toward my house.

I opened the door slowly, hoping to not wake my mother or father, but it didn't matter—my father was already awake. He sat promptly in his recliner, sipping a can of piss-poor beer and talking to the television. If I hadn't shut the door, I'm not sure he would've noticed me come inside. He glanced at me, and for the first time in years, he did a double take.

"Why are you wet?" He asked.

I sighed. "It's a long story." I kept walking. I always kept walking. There was never a reason for me to stay in the living room and as far as I was concerned there never would be. I made it to the kitchen before I realized I hadn't eaten since lunch. I was too tired to make myself dinner, though—even the microwave kind. I sat at the kitchen table and tried to let my body relax. It was difficult to say the least. I watched a spot on the table build up with water that dripped from my hair. It provided a soft thump against the old placemat.

"What are you doing?" I heard a voice from the kitchen. I jerked upward, startled.

"I didn't mean to scare you, kid," my dad said, opening the refrigerator. He pulled out two bottles of beer, popped their tops, and sat down at the table with me. I eyed him suspiciously; I couldn't remember the last time we'd sat at the table together.

"You look like you had a bad night," he said.

I nodded.

"You out drinkin'?" he asked.

I shook my head.

"Did someone hit you?" he asked, glaring at my nose.

"It was an accident. So was falling in my friend's pool," I said.

He laughed and shook his head. "Well, nights could be a whole lot worse, kid. I'll tell you that." With that, he pushed forward one of the bottles.

I glared at him as if he had just told a bad joke.

"Tonight's the first night you've ever gone out and stayed out for a while. Now, I know it looks like we don't pay attention to you much around here, but there's a reason for that. There's a method to the madness your mother and I ensue," he said and paused, as if he expected it to be so obvious to me.

"What's that?" I finally asked.

"We don't have to pretend there isn't an elephant in the room, kid. We're bad parents. At least, we're unfit parents. The only real way for us to be good parents is to not be parents at all," he said.

"That doesn't make any sense," I replied.

"Well, you're young. The world is still fairly black and white. Wait until you've aged—some gray starts to slip in there somewhere," he started. "But, so far, you've done a pretty good job on your own. You're more responsible than either of us ever were…that's for sure. And look at you, on a Friday night, your first night at a party, at least that's what I'm assuming, you come home sober as a judge. That's not how your mother and I operate so, kudos to you, kiddo. But tonight, I started to worry that maybe you hadn't had enough experience at home before stepping out into the real world. I know it's unorthodox but if you're going to drink, I want you to at least get your taste buds wet here, first," he said, nonchalantly.

"I don't drink'," I said, rolling my eyes.

"Maybe you don't, and maybe it's just a 'you don't drink yet' situation. Either way, drinking for the first time is like shooting a shotgun for the first time. If you go into it without knowing what's going to happen…you're going to fall hard. So, at least get those taste buds wet," he insisted.

I sighed and glared at the bottle. The irony was not lost upon me. The entire evening's disarray of disappointment, from Isis's to mine, all occurred because my morals were too high to condone drinking. All I could imagine was one day being my father in that easy chair, sipping his life away. Yet despite how hard I worked against that goal at the party, I still found myself, hours later, sitting at a kitchen table with my alcoholic father as he pushed a cold beer on his fourteen-year-old daughter. No, the irony was not lost upon me. As I picked up that bottle, pressed the glass opening to my lips, and sipped my first taste of alcohol; the irony was not lost upon me at all.

# Confession

"Is Isis home?" I asked as Jonathan answered the door the next morning.

He smiled and welcomed me inside. "I'm sure she's around here somewhere, Sam. Please come in."

Jonathan was as happy as always. He didn't seem upset about last night's situation at all. Perhaps, I thought as I walked toward Isis's bedroom, DJ had allowed the previous night's events go without telling their father. That seemed like something DJ would do for her—always protective.

I passed by the kitchen and, to my discomfort, saw Elliot the house guest sitting at the table, shirtless, cracking open a peanut. I kept moving forward but I didn't go unnoticed by Elliot.

"Pretty day today," Elliot said.

I stopped, being polite and nodded. "Yes, it is."

"You girls were out pretty late last night," he interjected.

Of course, I was caught off guard. I stuttered and broke my eye contact with him. "Yeah, I guess we were," I admitted.

Elliot dumped the broken peanuts into his mouth and crunched down on them. "Stayed out of trouble, I hope," he muttered through his full mouth.

"We did," I said quickly. I moved on; I couldn't stand being in that kitchen any longer.

"I just think you girls should be careful…you never know who you can trust," he said with an unsettlingly smile.

I smiled, nodded politely, and exited the kitchen feeling a cool chill shiver up my spine. I knocked on Isis's closed door—no response. "Isis, it's me…Sam." There was nothing. I knocked several more times but there was no answer.

"She's not going to answer you," I heard DJ's voice boom from behind me.

I turned around startled but, pleasantly surprised. "Oh," I said.

"She's not going to answer right now," DJ said, assuredly. "She hasn't answered anyone all morning."

"Oh," I said. My disappointment must have been obvious to him along with my embarrassment for calling him the night before.

"Are you alright?" he asked.

"I am."

"You don't look alright," he retorted.

I darted my eyes over to the kitchen. I couldn't see Elliot but I could hear his continuous crunching.

"Let's talk outside," DJ said.

We walked onto the back porch. DJ made himself comfortable by leaning up against the railing. I stood a foot or so away from him—doing the same.

"I wish he would leave," DJ blurted out.

"You really don't like him," I said, trying to remain impartial.

DJ shook his head. "He's…invasive. He's annoying. He…" DJ hesitated. It was clear there was more to it than awkwardness and annoyance.

"What is it?" I asked.

"He makes us feel weird. He makes Isis feel weird. I can tell. I don't know what it is exactly, but she doesn't like him. I don't like him. And Mom wouldn't have liked him either," he stated.

It was the first time I'd heard DJ mention his mother since

she passed away. Isis was always clear to me that she shouldn't be mentioned around her brother. He took it hard. Perhaps he took it harder than the rest of them. I didn't say anything; I didn't know what to say.

"He mocks things about Dad that our mother loved. He mocks things in this house that our mother loved. He mocks her very existence by staying here. Our mother wouldn't have wanted him here at all," DJ said.

"Why is he still here?" I asked, stupidly.

DJ shrugged his shoulders. "Beats me. Something about his house not being ready to move in yet. I don't know."

"I guess…that's why Isis didn't want to be here last night. I guess that's why she wanted to stay at Carly's." I said, feeling guilty.

"You were just trying to do the right thing. You were trying to protect Isis. I would have done the same thing. Protecting this family, like our mom did—that's what I care about," DJ said.

I smiled. "You're a good brother," I said, gazing at him.

"I try," he said. He smiled at me and I would almost have said he gazed back into my eyes. There was a brief moment with him, on that porch, that I didn't feel like an awkward fourteen-year-old girl. I felt like a woman. A woman who knew what she wanted and knew where life was going to take her.

"Sam," Isis's voice jogged us of our stare. She stood by the doors of the back porch, eyeing us both intently.

"Sam was just looking for you," DJ said.

"Come on," Isis said, motioning for me to come in the house.

I gave DJ another look and a brief smile, and followed my best friend back into her home.

"What are you doing?" she snapped at me.

"Checking on you," I stated.

She scoffed and folded her arms.

"What's your problem?" I asked.

"It looked like you were flirting with him," she said, pointing toward DJ, who remained on the back porch.

I felt my face grow warm and my skin began to itch—which always happened when I was nervous. I just hoped that I didn't betray myself by displaying every shade of red on my face. "I wasn't" I said weakly.

"Coulda fooled me," she said.

"I came to check on you after last night," I restated.

"I'm fine. And I was fine last night until you ruined it," she said.

I'd never seen Isis so upset with me. Her eyes cut through me like a knife through hot butter. It wasn't until that moment that I realized she was still wearing the same clothes from last night. A purple top, with a button-down flannel t-shirt over it, jeans with holes at the knees, and boots—her usual tomboyish attire, although the flannel was new. I could still smell the vodka on her.

"I'm sorry I got assaulted," I snapped.

Isis sighed and her eyes hung low. "I'm sorry," she breathed. "I'm sorry for snapping. And I'm sorry for leaving you alone," she admitted. "Let's go for a walk."

A few minutes later, I followed Isis into the wood behind our houses. Undoubtedly we were heading for her favorite pine.

"What happened last night?" she asked.

"Guy Garrison happened," I replied.

Isis grimaced. "Who invited that clown?"

"Wasn't it your party?" I questioned.

Isis shook her head, almost shamefully. "It was Carly's party. I just begged her to have it."

"Why?" I asked but Isis only shrugged.

I followed Isis as I always do. I knew the way to the pine; we'd walked it countless times, but I always allowed Isis to guide the way. I would let her figure out the path with the least amount of briers and branches to dodge and I would let her be the one to keep an extra eye out for bugs or snakes. Usually, Isis would march straight through the wood and directly to the pine without wavering either way, never letting the wood dominate her. Today, however, was different. Isis didn't take her most direct route and instead began to serpentine through the trees. I followed blindly as I always did, yet I couldn't help but question her motives.

"Are we going to the pine?" I asked.

"Eventually," she muttered, not really paying attention to me.

"What happened last night?" I asked. I didn't mean to blurt out the question. I didn't even intend on asking it but before I knew it, the words were flying out of my mouth.

Isis took several seconds before even uttering a sound. I thought I'd made her mad all over again but she finally looked toward me with a small smirk.

"I was being an idiot," she said.

"I'll be the judge of that," I said, playfully, feeling more comfortable with the subject matter now that I knew Isis wasn't going to attack me again.

"Cory and I started making out…It was great at first. Then…I don't know. He made a move, I freaked, backed up, tripped, knocked over the lamp, and stood awkwardly in the corner of the room," she said.

"Did you not want him to?" I asked.

"I wanted him to…at the time. Then when it happened, I didn't," Isis said.

There was a long period where neither of us said anything. That's the way it was sometimes, deep in the wood. We didn't always need noise. Actually, Isis didn't always need noise. That's part of why she preferred the timberline over the skyline. On the other hand, I would've rather heard anything to break the tension of the situation.

"Do you know Robert Frost?" I asked, trying to change the conversation.

"I think. The writer, right? A poet?" Isis questioned.

I nodded. "He wrote this poem, 'The Road Less Traveled.' It's one of my favorites," I said.

"How does it go?" Isis inquired.

I shook my head. "I don't remember all of it. I just remember the last stanza. 'Two paths diverge in the wood. And

I—I took the road less traveled. And it has made all the difference,'" I recited.

A hint of a smile hit Isis's face. "I like it."

"Like I said, one of my favorites," I stated.

"I like the ending. He chose a path and it made a difference. He didn't do what everyone else did. He got out of his slump and made it," Isis added.

I shrugged. "Is that what he's saying? Maybe he is saying the road less traveled is less traveled for a reason."

Her movement slowed. She kept her head down as she walked over the figs that crunched and broke beneath her feet.

"Are you okay?" I asked.

"I'm fine," she snapped.

We walked for a few more minutes in silence. Obviously my Frost poetry didn't have the positive effect I hoped it would have on her. We crept closer to the pine but I knew that if Isis had been determined, she would be there already. I wasn't complaining—I hated climbing the pine. I never felt safe and I never felt good at it. A twig snagged on my skirt. In that moment, I realized I had forgotten what to wear to the woods and it made me realize how long it had been since Isis had dragged me there.

"Why haven't we been out here in a while?"

"I don't know...we just haven't," Isis replied.

"It's your favorite place...I mean you wrote that po—"

"I just haven't, Sam," she barked at me.

I stopped moving. My feet were firmly planted atop twigs, branches, and grass. Isis continued to walk a few more feet before she realized I wasn't right behind her. She stopped and turned around, eyeing me—as if I'd lost my mind. "What are you doing?" she asked.

"I'm not walking another step until you tell me what's going on," I demanded.

Isis rolled her eyes and motioned me forward. "Come on, Sam."

"No," I protested.

"I actually do want to get to the pine sometime, today," she remarked.

"Then talk to me," I pleaded, still refusing to budge from my spot.

It was a scary thing—at least at the time. I'd never stood up to Isis in such a way. I never had to, either. Isis might've been the alpha dog of the two of us…but she always took care of me. I never felt like I was beneath her. Not until she began to change. Isis glared at me for a long time. She wasn't waiting for me to speak—but she wasn't saying anything either. She just glared. Her green eyes peered into mine for what seemed like an hour. I did everything I could to keep eye contact. It was like looking into the sun without blinking. It was almost impossible and when you achieved it you nearly felt tears forming in your eyes.

"I'm not doing this with you Sam," she said.

"Too bad. You have to. It's what friends do. You've been acting so strangely for weeks. I can't keep ignoring it, Isis. Friends talk to each other. If you don't want to talk to me. If you don't want to let me know what's going on in your life then maybe we're not really friends anymore" I said, knowing, even then, how childish it sounded.

"Some things you just don't want to talk about, Sam. Can't you just…I don't know, be there for me anyway?" She said. Her voice cracked and I heard the uneasiness in her tone. I wasn't the only one fighting tears.

"I've tried, Isis. All it gets me is my best friend snapping at me, getting knocked in the face by jerks, and being pushed into a pool. I drank a beer with my dad that night. My dad. Whatever you're going through, whatever is making you change, It's starting to affect my life, too. If you can't even give me a reason for that…I don't see what I'm doing out here—in the middle of the woods," I explained.

It felt like a barbell being lifted off of my chest. It hurt to say every word—but not saying it hurt worse. I shook my head, after a few seconds, when I realized she wasn't going to reply, turned around, and started walking back toward civilization. I made it a few feet—a few lonely, scary, feet—before I heard her voice echo through the wood.

"Sam!" she exclaimed, her voice nearly destroyed.

I could hear tears in her cry. I turned around and my suspicion was confirmed. Isis was weeping openly. I walked to her as fast as I could and grasped her arms.

"What is it? What is it, Isis?" I asked.

"He…" she started. She had begun to sob—and hearing her words proved to grow more difficult as each one passed.

"What is it?" I repeated.

"He…what he does," she started, through broken sobs. "He comes in my room, from down the hall, and…he…" her voice broke again.

Cold chills shivered down my spine. Though her voice broke, I didn't need to hear the conclusion to know what was happening. My heart sank to my stomach and then twisted in a knot. Tears were flowing freely from my eyes now. I felt them drop off my cheeks.

"And he. He. He," she kept saying like she was broken record. That's what Isis looked to me, in that moment— broken. And I had no idea how to put the pieces back together. I grabbed her, and embraced her in a hug. She collapsed into my arms and chest and sobbed louder. Her body shook. So did mine.

"Who did this, Isis? Who?" I asked. "Was it him? Was it Elliot?"

Her sobs grew louder and I held her tighter. I didn't need her to confirm it. I knew what had happened. I had no words of comfort. I had no form of action. All I had was Isis in my arms—and I wasn't about to let go. We didn't make it to the pine that day. In fact, we never made it back. Not at the same time, anyway—not as children. Something told me, even then, that life was too complicated now for tree climbing. That was something done by children. Standing in the wood, embracing Isis, I saw no children. I heard no children.

# Help

"I need help. My friend was raped." The words seemed unrealistic as soon as they exited my mouth. As if I were entrapped in a bad dream that was repeating in a loop. It had felt that way ever since Isis told me what happened to her. We stayed in the wood for an hour. I held her whilst she cried. I cried, too. She could never calm down long enough to give me the details but I didn't need them. I jumped straight to the only point I knew I had to make—that she needed help.

"Absolutely not," she said when I first mentioned it. It caused her to slow her breath and cease the tears, if only momentarily. I suggested talking to her father. She rebelled drastically against that idea. I couldn't blame her. I tried to imagine what it would be like to tell my father that his best friend was abusing me. I couldn't bring those words to my mouth—and my father was barely present in my life. I couldn't fathom how Isis's father, Jonathan, would react to such news. And I couldn't imagine Isis bringing herself to admit it to him, either.

The only help I knew I could lend, at the time, was my home. I told Isis that day as we walked passed the trees and into my backyard, that I wouldn't let her spend another night alone.

"We can't get away with that," she said, drying her eyes. Her voice was tiresome and dull. It was a horrible sound—a sound as if she had already given up. We walked to the bus stop again. It was Saturday, so of course, we weren't waiting on the school bus but a free city bus would come by every thirty minutes or so. We waited for nearly that long, if not longer, before the bus came. We rode around for an hour. She just stared out the window and would comment every now and then about something or another she saw. I entertained her the best I could but it was pointless. It was as if getting her to admit it, opened something up within her and now she was suddenly expressing emotions she'd been ignoring. I wanted to ask her more questions. I wanted to find out exactly what that terrible house guest was doing to her so I knew what to say when I begged someone for help. I knew that I couldn't ask though. I knew I never would ask and I knew she would never tell me.

"You have to tell someone, you know. Someone other than myself," I finally said after I built the courage to redirect us to the conversation. We were no longer on the bus, but walking down Main Street, each with a milkshake in tow. Isis didn't reply. "You can't just wait for him to leave," I added.

Isis took a sip of her milkshake and refused once again to answer me.

"Isis—all you have to do is ask for help," I stressed.

"Leave it alone, Sam," she said, nervously.

"No," I said, firmly.

We walked to the square—it was small and had several shops circling around a courthouse. It wasn't the city but it was a lot closer.

"If you don't, I will," I said, and this caught her attention. She eyed me for several seconds, surveying my tone and expression. She knew I was telling the truth. I think she respected how firm I was being—that's the only reason she didn't yell at me.

"Talking about it will only cause more problems," she said as if it was obvious.

"That's fear talking," I said. Of course, I wasn't educated much on the subject of sexual abuse. No fourteen-year-old I knew was properly educated. In fact, I'm not sure my parents were properly educated either. Anytime I remember hearing my father say something about whatever rapist the news media was covering, he would always sigh and say something obscene or something insensitive: "Women should know better than to be in places they could get raped" or "She shouldn't have flirted with him so much." Looking back, the words he said made me cringe. I've often wondered if my mother felt just as bothered by his words

After an hour or two of persisting, I finally convinced Isis that she should go to someone. I suggested that we go straight to the police station but she refused. She said if anything, she'd talk to a counselor at school.


"I need help. My friend was raped." I had just spoken this heinous sentence to Mrs. Oates, on an irregular scheduled appointment that following Monday. Her blue eyes grew another size at least, her lips parted and all of the color from her face seemed to fade away.

"Sam," her voice trembled as she spoke. I waited for her to grasp the gravity of the situation at hand and become professional again. She cleared her throat and blinked for too long, attempting to compose herself. "Tell me what is going on," she said.

I sighed. I had something else in mind when I told Isis she should talk to someone. I never thought I would be the one telling someone what happened to her. I assumed Isis would want to do that—but she refused. She told me almost directly, that if help was to be sought, I would have to be her voice.

"I have a friend, and…there's this man staying in her house. And, he's going into her room at night…" my voice trailed off. I'd gotten Isis to give me the bare minimum of detail for me to relate it to an adult. I didn't expect being the messenger would be this hard. It made me wonder how Isis brought herself to even tell me—her best friend. "He comes into her room at night. And, well. He makes her do things," I finally said.

Mrs. Oates's pen was moving rapidly across a notepad. "Can you tell me what things?" she asked.

I wanted to yell in her face. I wanted to storm out and leave. I had no idea how she could've been so bold to ask such an obvious and invasive question like that one. I refrained from being argumentative and tried to collect my words through gritted teeth. "Sexual things. He makes her touch him. He touches her. If she doesn't—he forces her. And then he forces her to…" I trailed off again. "He forces her to have sex with him."

"How does he force her, Sam?" Mrs. Oates asked again, scribbling drastically with her pen.

"I don't know. He just does," I said, feeling uneasy.

She nodded her head slowly and continued writing. "Who is your friend, Sam?" she asked.

I hesitated. Although I knew it was important that she knew Isis's name to in order to help her, I also knew that Isis was terrified of giving her name to Mrs. Oates.

"I don't know if she wants me to say," I said, cautiously.

"I need to know the name if I am going to help her, Sam," Mrs. Oates said, calmly.

I nodded. I thought about my options. I wished Isis had come with me. I wished Isis had the courage to do what I scarcely had the courage to do. But, when I watched her cry and shake, I knew that if it were me in her shoes and her in mine, she'd stop at nothing to give me all the help I needed.

"Isis Cassidy," I stated.

Mrs. Oates looked up from her notepad and made eye contact with me. Glaring—as if she just now realized I was admitting something horrible to her. There was a pause where I expected her to speak but she didn't say anything. Suddenly, I could smell the scented candle that sat on her desk. I could feel my legs sticking to the brown, ugly leather seat in which I sat. I jolted my foot, slowly, up and down on the rough carpet. I couldn't stand the silence. I couldn't stand the staring.

"Isis," she said as if she hoped she'd heard me incorrectly.

"Isis," I unfortunately confirmed.

She resumed to her notepad and I took a sigh of relief from the unbelievable tension.

"I really wish I could hear this from Isis," Mrs. Oates said laying her pen down on the notepad and intertwining her fingers. She looked at me, waiting for a response; she waited to hear me give a justifiable reason why it wasn't Isis sitting in that brown, ugly, skin-sticking leather chair, instead of me.

"She wanted to," I started in a lying defense. "She's scared. I told her I would help her."

Mrs. Oates smiled. Her smile was captivating. It was jubilant but it was also innocent. "Sweetie," she said, in a smooth voice. "What happened to your nose?"

I didn't understand. Yes, my nose and mouth were still bruised from the conflict between Guy and Colin but I didn't understand, at first, what it had to do with Isis.

"Some guys were messing around. I got caught in the crossfire," I admitted with a shrug. It was the truth and I told it as such. Still, Mrs. Oates pondered as she propped her elbows on the wooden desk. "

"No one hit you?" she asked, studying my face.

"Not on purpose," I argued.

"It's certainly a nasty bruise. Did you bleed?" she questioned.

I sighed. "What does this have to do with Isis or the fact that she's being raped by her dad's friend?" I finally snapped. I don't know how loud my question was but by judging the look on Mrs. Oates's face as she adjusted herself in her chair and cut her eyes over to the door, I assumed it was loud enough that others might hear.

"I'm just making sure I have all the facts straight, Sam," she said in a murmured voice.

It wasn't until that moment that I realized what she was doing. I grimaced and rolled my eyes at the same time. "I'm not the one being raped. It really is Isis," I insisted.

"I know, I know," Mrs. Oates said as if she never insinuated an alternative. "I'm just checking on you, Sam. I know your father can do some heinous things when he's been drinking…"

her voice trailed off and I felt my skin burn as it itched for me to leap out of my chair and across her desk.

I was always the first person to admit that my father was not really a father at all. I would not stand for him to be called anything near a rapist, however. The man didn't even hug me.

"My dad is not doing that to me!" I shouted. I felt my nose flare and my ears burn.

"Sam, I was only trying to—"

"I came here to talk to you about Isis. She needs help. She needs you, or someone—anyone. She has to get out of that house or that man needs to get out of that house," I protested.

"Who is this man, Sam?" she asked.

I sighed. "His name is Elliot...that's all I know. Or all I can remember. He's a friend of Jonathan, Isis's dad," I said.

"And you say he's staying with them?" she asked taking me more serious this time.

I nodded. I watched her jot viciously on a piece of paper. I felt relief. Mrs. Oates removed her glasses and smiled at me. Her teeth were exponentially white; the kind of white you see actors have in all the movies. That's what she looked like— something from a movie. I only hoped it would end like most of those movies—with a happy ending.

"Thank you for sharing. It was very brave of you, Sam. I'll report this at once," Mrs. Oates said, reassuringly.

"Thank you," I quickly said.

"But you know...if Isis needs to talk about this, she can come to me, too," the counselor added.

I nodded my head. "She knows."

"Sam...are you sure everything is okay at home?" Mrs. Oates asked, and it was clear to me as her less-than-genuine smile softened to a gentler toothless one, that when I said "Isis" she heard "Sam." I picked up my backpack and walked toward the door.

"Sam, you still have twenty more minutes," Mrs. Oates stated, perched behind her large wooden desk. "Twenty more minutes to talk about anything you want to talk about," she said.

I shook my head. "No, it's not about me anymore. It's only about Isis."

Despite leaving Mrs. Oates's office twenty minutes early from our weekly scheduled appointment, I was still ten minutes late arriving to Mr. Croft's English class. He waved me in without hearing a word of the lie that I had prepared: My session ran long because of a phone call Mrs. Oates received. Instead, I had been in the library researching ways I could help Isis, because I didn't have a good feeling about the conversation I had with Mrs. Oates.

I had stowed away in one of the computer cubicles in the library, which I often did when I had a chance—mainly because my parents were spending too much money on alcohol to even consider the possibility of fitting the cost of a computer into the budget. The research came up pretty dry. I found hotlines and counselors and several church organizations that tended to rape victims—but they were only options available for Isis if she would be vocal. And that was the problem. Even if Mrs. Oates did follow through with reporting the rape, I was afraid Isis would never find the courage to openly admit what had happened.

I took my seat beside Isis, who watched me nervously. "Did you talk to her?" she asked, before I had the chance to greet her. I nodded my head and was able to see the physical burden fade away from Isis's face. She didn't smile. She didn't even look relieved. She looked...accomplished.

"I think things would go a lot smoother if you talked to her, though," I whispered.

Isis frowned. She eyed Mr. Croft, who hadn't slowed down his lecture about Hamlet to address my tardiness or the fact that two of his students who sat near the front of the class whispered idly to one another.

"Why?" she finally asked, her eyebrows crunching atop her green eyes.

"She thought I was talking about myself," I stressed.

"But you told her it was me?" she asked quickly.

"Yes."

Isis didn't look relieved, or disappointed. She looked scared. I smiled at her and nodded my head. "It's going to be okay."


As class ended, and I gathered my things to follow Isis out the door when Mr. Croft grabbed my attention.

"Can I speak to you, Sam?" he asked, coolly.

I sighed and motioned for Isis to leave without me. The rest of my classmates filed out slowly and Mr. Croft waited patiently for each one to leave before even looking toward me. When the last kid, Jimmy Johnson, who was notorious for sleeping through his classes, slugged his way out the door, Mr. Croft turned to me.

"Little late today, Sam," he said as he rounded the edge of his desk and plopped down in an old worn out green desk chair.

"I'm sorry, Mr. Croft. My session with Mrs. Oates went over a little. She had a phone call," I lied.

Mr. Croft waved his hand. "I don't care about that and not just because you're lying," he said. Mr. Croft was a middle-aged man, with thin black hair that had already begun to gray at the temples. He always seemed to have a stubble of facial hair and despite his slender build, he always carried himself like he was overweight and slow-moving.

"My real question is more personal," he added in a more serious tone than before.

It always made me nervous when adults used serious tones with me or with anyone. An adult with a serious tone has never lead to anything positive.

"How are things Sam? I don't mean academically. I mean outside of here. Out there, where it matters," he said gesturing his head toward his window—his only representation of what the real world might be like to someone inside the classroom.

His window faced the baseball field, however and despite spending several nights watching my dad drink and piss himself in front of a television screen while watching baseball game after baseball game, I never once found it to be an experience I'd call realistic.

"Things are…fine," I said, hesitantly.

"With you? Things with you are fine?"

"Yes."

"And Isis?" he asked. His eyes were unwavering—a tight lipped stare. He was serious.

I shook my head. "No," I said, truthfully. He nodded. I think he understood even before I answered that I would respond in that way. He was a keen observer. He leaned forward and picked up a large ball made exclusively out of rubber bands. He picked at one of the rubbery blue straps that laced over a red band. He flicked it against the leathery ball, as if he were suddenly too nervous to talk, or look me in the eye.

"Anything you want to talk about?" he asked.

I shook my head.

"Anything about Isis you want to tell me?"

I shook my head.

"Nothing?" he said and sighed. He picked up the rubber band ball and bounced it up and down for a few moments. I hesitated to ask what he wanted me for—but it was obvious by that point. Mr. Croft's eyes softened though. He smiled a weak smile and before I knew what was happening, he cornered me with the second most awkward question he could ask.

"Is there something going on with Isis, personally? At home, maybe?"

"I can't really say." My eyes drifted as the words slipped out of my mouth.

Mr. Croft nodded his head. "It's just…I know you're her best friend. I know you care about her. I know you love her. It's obvious, Sam. You do care a lot about her. It's also obvious that something is happening to her."

I tilted my head in confusion. Of course I could see the differences in Isis; she was my best friend. I knew her like the skin on my hand. To find that our English teacher had just as much insight seemed unrealistic.

"Her grades have declined. Her work ethic is not what it used to be. Her poetry…is still good, but its content has shifted dramatically," he explained. His eyes locked on mine as if his sentence was a passcode to unearth buried secrets. I only shrugged my shoulders.

"I've talked to her and I've tried to schedule a parent-teacher conference. If it's something personal that she'd rather not discuss with me—I understand. My only concern at this point is her safety," he said and pressed his propped elbows against the table.

"I'm going to miss my bus," I said hesitating for the door.

"I just want to help," he said smoothly.

It was a comfort to hear such sincerity coming from someone else who cared about Isis. I believed Mrs. Oates when she said she'd look into it. The obvious truth, however, is that still after hearing everything I said, she was more concerned about me than she ever was about Isis. It didn't make sense to me but I certainly recognized it.

"Sam if there's something going on, then an adult needs to know. It doesn't have to be me but she needs to tell someone," Mr. Croft stated.

I nodded my head. "Someone knows," I said.

"Is something being done about it?" he asked, his eyes glaring through me.

I sighed. It was suddenly easier to be honest than deceitful. "I hope so, Mr. Croft," I said. His jaw tightened and he rubbed one palm over a clinched fist rubbing his knuckles individually; that's when he asked the most awkward question he could've asked me.

"If Isis is being sexually assaulted at home, please tell me that an adult outside of her family knows?" he asked.

My heart sank. I was both relieved and terrified. I wasn't sure why I was so scared when he finished his sentence but my legs shook and my voice trembled as I replied: "Mrs. Oates. She knows. How—how do you know?"

He sighed and stood up from his desk. His eyes were wider now and I caught their shimmer from the other side of the desk—he was crying.

"Because I know a victim when I see one," his voice broke halfway through the sentence. He cleared his throat and sniffed. "Good. I'm glad Mrs. Oates knows. Thank you, Sam."

As I left Mr. Croft's classroom and joined the mass of students walking toward the busses, whilst keeping my eye out for Isis, I realized that not all of Mr. Croft's tears were for her. Some of those tears, maybe most of those tears, were for someone else. Someone he knew that went through the same thing—maybe even himself. It was a daunting thought. A thought I had never dared to think before but couldn't stop thinking about now in the common room among all my classmates. How many people among me had suffered something as horrible as Isis had been suffering? How many of them laughed on the outside and cried in someone else's bed every night? How many of them had someone they could talk to about it? How many of them didn't? How many victims stood elbow to elbow with me? How many offenders did, also?


Isis and I sat in my room that night eating a couple of frozen dinners I microwaved for us. I still refused to let her go home for very long—only now and again so her father wouldn't think of her missing and to slowly bring more of her belongings over. After the sun went down, I refused to let her leave my sight. We spent the meal talking about everything other than what was festering on the forefronts of our brains—that at any moment a police officer would be knocking on the Cassidys' door looking for Elliot, asking questions and hopefully, making an arrest.

Admittedly, it was nice to talk about something else for a change. I'd spent so much time trying to pry the truth out of her that when I did, it seemed there was no other topic in which we found solace.

"I saw Emerson checking you out today," Isis said, smirking a little as she picked at her once frozen macaroni and cheese.

I blushed. "If Emerson was checking me out it was only

because he was comparing my stickily structure to your…not-so-stickily structure," I teased.

She laughed. "Don't be so down on yourself."

"What about you? Are you and Cory…" my voice trailed off. Neither one of us had mentioned him since the party.

Her smile faded for a moment. She poked her food with her fork, stabbing one noodle at a time. "I don't know," she finally let out. "I—I think I scared him at the party."

"What happened?" I asked boldly.

"Nothing," she was quick to say. "Well…I mean we made out. It was getting intense, I guess. Before I knew it we were in a bedroom. I dragged him there, though. He seemed really uncomfortable but he was so sweet about it. Then I just…I don't know—freaked. I've sorta been avoiding him ever since that night," she admitted, hanging her head.

"I think he really likes you," I said, as upbeat as I could manage.

She smiled and nodded her head. "Yeah, I think he probably does." Her smile was an ever quick fade, though, as were most of them. The truth of the matter, at least what appeared to be the truth from where I was standing was that although she liked Cory, a part of herself hated him. A part of Isis hated every man now despite the fact it only took one to harm her.

"Why did Mr. Croft ask you to stay after class today?" she asked again. She'd first asked me when I caught up with her on the bus. I shrugged it off and started an entirely different conversation. When she revisited the question in the middle of my bedroom floor, I had no subject in which to transfer our attention.

"You," I admitted when I knew my face had already given me away.

"What did you say? What did he say?" she asked quickly. "Please tell me you didn't tell him anything you told Mrs. Oates?"

I shook my head and waved my hands. "Hey, calm down. No, I didn't tell him anything like that," I lied, feeling incredibly guilty as I did so. It was suddenly easier to be more deceitful than honest. I didn't know what she could handle—and I honestly didn't want to find out.

It was just after Isis had calmed down from her slight shock of fear, when we heard a pounding on the front door. My father cursed at my mother to answer the door. She cursed back reminding him she was a wife—not a slave. We softened our voices to whispers and listened impatiently.

There were murmurs at the front door. I could hear my dad slur his words and I was almost positive that saliva was dripping from his lip as he wiped it on his stained wife beater. Another voice stressed a little louder and clearer, rumbled through the walls. I heard a faint gasp echo into my ear.

"That's my dad," Isis said, her whisper breaking as her sentence ended. She leapt off my bedroom floor and darted out the doorway.

"Wait!" I called after her—trying to catch up. I was afraid of the worst, that Jonathan would be standing there with Elliot beside him looking for answers to serious questions I didn't want answered in front of my parents. Isis rounded the corner through the kitchen and into the living room. She halted in the entry way and I quickly approached her side. Jonathan was standing at the front door as my father hung onto it. Elliot was not beside him. Instead, it was a police officer. A sparkle of hope arose in my chest.

"Isis Cassidy?" the officer spoke. Isis nodded. "May we talk to you outside? Privately?"

I smiled half-heartedly. I was nervous, but I knew that Jonathan would be supportive. He might've loved his best friend—but he loved his own child more. Still, the tightened lips and the flexed jaw that seemed carved on Jonathan made me feel uncomfortable.

"Please Isis. We need to sort this mess out," Jonathan stated. I didn't like how he called it a mess—as if it was an accident, as if Isis had been clumsy.

"We don't have to—I know why you're here," Isis started and moved toward the door. "It's not true," she said.

The words bounced off my ears like a bad joke. I laughed—

in a hysterical kind of way. Everyone in the room, including the police officer looked in my direction. My parents were confused—at least my father was confused; my mother seemed too drunk to really care as she mumbled inappropriate comments about the police officer's handsome looks.

"What's going on?" I asked as I ignored everyone's gaze—everyone's but Isis's.

"I said it's not true, Sam," she said in a snarled tone. "I don't know whose sick idea of a joke this was, Sam, but it's not true—I haven't been raped," she said, coldly.

I shook my head in disbelief but she only turned her back on me. The room was quiet—passed quiet. My father let go of the door and stood on his own two feet looking more sober than I'd seen him in weeks.

"Let's go, Isis," Jonathan said, looking embarrassed and disturbed as he placed his hand on her shoulder and guided her out our front door.

"No," I said to myself more than them as I followed quickly behind. I heard both of my parents call my name but I ignored them. I made it out into the grass of my front yard before I yelled Isis's name loud enough for her, the police officer, and Jonathan to turn around.

"YOU KNOW THAT'S NOT TRUE, ISIS. YOU CAN'T BACK DOWN NOW," I screamed.

"Sam!" my father yelled as he ran outside joining me on the lawn.

Isis shook her head. "Stop it, Sam," she said.

"I WON'T!"

She didn't listen to me though. She turned around and without another word for either of us, she walked off of my lawn and onto hers. I moved forward but felt a jerk pull be back. My father had his arm around my torso and his free hand on my head attempting to calm me down.

"Shh, Pumpkin. Calm down," he muttered. I tried to break his grasp but, of course, I couldn't. I could smell the stench of alcohol on his breath. I could smell it through his shirt along with the minty smell of Winston Light cigarettes. As he held me and I watched my best friend walk into a dark house where I knew someone was there to harm her, where she would be in danger, out of reach from help; I thought about what I contemplated in Mrs. Oates's office.

I realized that maybe help wasn't coming for Isis. I realized that no matter what I had wanted—this wasn't a movie. As I saw the door slam shut behind her, I realized it wasn't a movie at all.

# The Plan

I didn't speak to Isis for the next three days. She skipped most of her classes and the times she was present, she gave me the cold shoulder. I couldn't express my anger. She'd completely betrayed me and yet I still hurt for her. Despite my feelings, my actions were the only thing anyone had paid attention to since that night. Jonathan, for example, avoided eye contact with me ever since, and my parents had muttered to each other about my lashing out for attention.

Later that night, after Isis had left with her dad and the police officer, my father came into my room and asked me about what happened. He was drunk, of course, but he was talkative. I told him the truth and he shook his head. He told me cliché sayings, that even at that age, I knew were cliché. "There are two sides to everything." "She could be looking for attention." I argued with him until he lost interest. But before he left my room he turned around, rubbed a finger in his ear, and burped.

"You know, I know that fella staying with them," he started. "He's a good man. A United States Marine—at least he used to be. Put it to bed, Sam. Who are they gonna believe? A teenage girl? Or a man who served his country?" With those terrifying words, my father staggered out of my room. It was the last true moment in my childhood that I ever remember feeling something toward my father. After that it was only numbness, but that night, it was anger and disrespect.

Three days later, I decided to break into my savings—which consisted of sixty-three dollars and some change in a shoebox under my bed. I felt utterly alone. And if I were going to feel such a way, I would feel that way in the city—at least for the afternoon. Summer had officially started and I found it bittersweet. Unlike most teenagers free for the summer, I was constantly worried about Isis.

I was walking down the road in front of my house to the bus stop, when I heard the roar of an engine rapidly approaching from behind. DJ sat behind the wheel of his dad's beat up pick-up truck and rolled to a stop when he reached me. He smiled. He wore a faded tank top and a baseball cap, and motioned for me to open the passenger door.

"Hey stranger," he said with a smile.

"Hey,' I replied, blushing nervously. I could see his jeans, ripped and cut in various places. He looked rugged, but clean, and that confused every bit of my fourteen-year-old brain.

"Where are you heading?" he asked.

"The city."

He grimaced and shook his head. "Now? Why?"

"I don't know. Just to get out," I replied.

"Traffic will be too bad in the city around this time."

"Well, I'm taking the bus, obviously."

"Oh, so you don't want to ride with me?" he asked as a smile stretching across his face.

My heart seemed to stop and then sped rapidly to catch up. "You want me to ride with you? To the city?"

"City, country, where-ever. It's a pretty day. We don't have to waste it in the city."

As much as I preferred the city over the country, I couldn't help but agree. The sun was high and a perfect breeze was making this particular day more beautiful than most. It didn't hurt that I was now in the company of DJ, someone with whom I'd rather spend my time despite the location.

We took a ride in the truck, which was louder than I had expected and left any chance of conversation in the cab to be next to pointless. We rode with the windows down and I let my arm hang limply out the window to allow the sun to gently kiss the top layer of my skin. I was so pale, I knew that I would burn by tomorrow but I didn't care. DJ on the other hand, had the same genes Isis did—which meant naturally tan skin. He was a shade lighter than Isis and his eyes were minty blue. Perhaps it was the infatuation of him that made me so certain but I could've sworn I'd never seen an eye color like that in my entire life.

We rode for what seemed like half an hour, but to be honest, I couldn't exactly tell the time. The radio's display in the truck's dash was broken and I was too busy trying not to look stupid to think about anything else. Finally, we ended up on a small dock by a lake. He told me he went there often to swim or fish or just sit and watch the landscape. Which is what we did that afternoon—watched the country around us.

"So you're not mad at me?" I finally asked after some nervous small talk. As much as I enjoyed the one-on-one with him, I wanted to know what was being said about me in the Cassidy house.

DJ shook his head, exhausting a short chuckle which seemed forced. "No."

"Isis sure is…and your dad, too," I muttered.

He picked up a small rock by the lake and skimmed it across the surface of the water. "I wouldn't worry too much about it, okay?" he said.

"Easy for you to say," I sighed.

"Is it true?" he finally said turning to me. His eyes glared at me. It was uncomfortable. "Did she really say someone was hurting her?" he asked.

It was hard to see the look of pity and worry across his face. My stomach twisted in a knot. I realized at that moment, DJ was the only one who believed me. I wanted to throw up for how I made him feel. Yet, I was relieved to be validated. I nodded my head and he looked down, away from me.

"I'm sorry," I uttered.

"Did she say who?" he barked.

"It's Elliot…"

DJ grimaced and looked away. I paused and waited for him to say something—anything. And when he did it was a string of profanity and violent promises. I winced, even flinching, when he began yelling into the empty space between us and the lake. When he noticed, he calmed down and collapsed beside me.

"I'm sorry for that," he said. I nodded.

"You love her," I replied.

He looked at me—almost shockingly. "Thank you for understanding."

"So do I."

"I know."

We sat silently on the dock for a while. Occasionally he would pick up a rock and lazily attempt to skim it across the water again but it never worked as well as the first try. Eventually, I picked a nearby Daisy and planted it behind my ear and let my hair weave around it.

"Irises are pretty," DJ said.

"It's a Daisy," I laughed.

DJ laughed too. "So I don't know flowers very well."

"At all, I would say," I teased. He pretended to throw a pebble at me. We spent the next hour talking and joking like that—occasionally touching on more serious topics. He asked me about my parents. What they were like and such. This was, of course, a subject I usually lied about—but not this time. I told him the truth. I explained to him how my parents drank themselves unconscious almost daily. I told them how they fought. He tried to comfort me.

"All parents fight."

"Not like mine."

I told him about the time I caught my father burning my mother's forearm with a cigarette. DJ grimaced and started to say hateful things about my father but I told him it was a direct response to her throwing a pot filled with boiling water at him.

DJ shook his head and sighed.

"I guess every family has their hiccups," he said.

I shrugged my shoulders. With the exception of his mother passing and an awful stranger lurking in their home, the Cassidys seemed like a perfect family. True, Jonathan was a bit spaced out most of the time and it didn't seem like they had much money. I suppose in some ways, all ways, their family had a little more than a hiccup. Realizing that fact, however, brought me no comfort…as I still envied it.

"So where do you see yourself going?" he asked me.

"Going?"

"You know. After high school. College? Are you gonna stay here? Move away?"

"The city."

"The city?" he questioned, with a scoff as he took a sit on the edge of the dock. "What is so great about that stupid city?"

"Everything, it's not here. I mean this town—not here. I like it here. This dock and stuff," I said, nervously. "I mean…I want to be a writer. And I want to be around people and exciting things and…anyway that's where people can be writers. The city. I can't be a writer here."

DJ nodded but didn't look at me. "The city is okay, I guess. I mean—it's not here. And I mean that in a negative sense. But, I guess I can see why you'd want to be there."

"What do you want to do?"

"I want to fix cars. You know, a mechanic," he said.

I smiled, brightly, at him. "I can see that. You're good at that. You'd make more in the city, though."

"There's no trees in the city. There's no mountains. I like the quietness the mountains give me," DJ said.

"You sound just like Isis," I chuckled, but soon both of our smiles wiped away.

"If what you told me is true," DJ uttered, "then you were only trying to help her."

I nodded, but was unable to speak. He patted the plank of wood beside him on the edge of the dock and I obliged by sitting next to him.

"You're a good friend," he murmured. His arm was relatively close to mine. I could feel the heat from his skin.

"I try," I said sheepishly.

"I see the way guys look at her," he started. I felt an uncomfortable knot twist in my stomach. "I see how they eye her in the hallways. When we go swimming here at the lake, sometimes a drifter or another farmer will come by. I see them all eye her. Eight-year-old boys to eighty-year-old perverts. I hate them," DJ said, intently. "I know I shouldn't. But I know what it's like to be a guy. To think the things we think," he said.

"Girls think things too," I said, defending equality the best I knew how.

"If you hadn't called me that night...that night of the party," he stated, shaking his head as he stared out onto the water. "I don't know what would've happened. You really are a good friend."

I smiled, nervously, and full of guilt as I felt that my sudden happiness came at Isis's expense. Would everything ever stop being at Isis's expense?


A little bit later we found ourselves back in the Cassidy's drive way and waiting for us, as DJ parked the truck was Isis. I leapt out of the pickup and walked toward her.

"Isis," I said.

She moved toward me with a stern and awful look upon her face. "What are you doing?"

"I just went to the dock with DJ," I said, perplexed at her attitude.

"What are you doing hanging out with him?" she questioned.

"Calm down, Isis," DJ said as he slammed the driver's side door.

I turned my attention back to Isis, whose ears were burning red and her nostrils flaring. "You can't just turn my brother into your boyfriend!"

It was my turn to turn red but from embarrassment.

"Umm, I'm going inside the house," DJ said.

It was easy to sense his embarrassment, too. He was probably embarrassed for me and wanted to get as far away as possible.

"I'm not turning anyone into my boyfriend!" I snapped at Isis.

She shook her head and walked around in a circle as if she were trying to calm herself down. "I told you there is a man in my house——" she paused just after her voice quivered. "And he's hurting me. And you're off…hanging out with my brother. Like it's no big deal what's happening here," she said.

"In case you forgot, I tried helping you. I tried getting the police involved and I tried to get you to tell them what happened but you wouldn't," I protested.

"I can't!" Isis blurted out.

"Why not?!"

"Because I can't! Okay?" she said angrily.

"No, no, it's not okay!" I yelled. "I've done everything I can think of Isis. I'm just a kid, too. Remember? And I don't—I don't know what to do anymore. If you won't talk to the police. If you won't let anyone help you…I don't know what to do."

Isis wiped a tear from her eye. Her bottom lip quivered and she wrapped her arms around herself. My heart broke, but my eyes stayed strongly locked onto her.

"I can't tell anyone…no one…no one would believe me," she muttered through her tears.

"I believe you."

"You have to believe me. You're my friend."

"DJ believes you."

"It doesn't matter, Sam!" she shouted.

I hesitated from yelling and tried to keep my cool. I approached her. The wind picked up and I felt a small chill dance through an otherwise warm day. The leaves in the trees danced on their branches and the blades of grass moved slowly like an old jazz song was just starting up. Isis's entire body shook like a wet cat that barely survived drowning but didn't know it yet.

"Is it because he's a soldier or something?" I asked.

Her shaking didn't cease, but she looked up at me. Her eyes were dead—hopelessly dead.

"I….my dad said something about him being a soldier."

"You told your dad this?" she said, her voice sliced like a knife.

"He heard what I yelled out to you as you left my house…my dad's a drunk not an idiot," I explained.

Isis didn't say anything. Instead, she let her eyes drop down to the dancing grass.

"If it's because he's a soldier or something…that doesn't matter, Sam. A police officer will believe you. You just gotta…you gotta tell them," I said.

"His word against mine," she uttered under her breath.

I sighed impatiently. "So what do you want to do?" I asked. She gazed up at me as if this was the question she'd been waiting to hear the entire time.

"I want to leave," she said with more excitement than I'd heard from her in weeks.

"What?"

"I want to leave, Sam. I want to get out of here. Run away—whatever you want to call it. But I want it. I want to leave," she said, again with enthusiasm.

"You…you can't just leave, Isis. He's the one that should be leaving."

"But he's not. He can't. I can. I'm leaving. I'm going to leave, I'm going to do this…and I want you to come with me," she said as she grasped my hand in her own.

My heart sank. I could nearly hear its beating echo in the pit of my stomach. "You—you want me to go with you?"

"Why not, Sam? You talk about leaving this dump all the time," she said.

"I don't know…"

"What's there to know? You hate it here. You wanna keep coming home to your mom and dad fighting? How about you walking in on them having sex again? You want to do that? You want your dad to get so drunk he grabs the closest thing for a punching bag? Do you want to wait until he starts doing that to you? Or has he already started?" she barked.

"Isis!" I said through tears.

She stopped and put her arms around me. "I'm sorry, Sam. I'm sorry...but you said it yourself. You want out. You want the city. Remember my dream, Sam? Remember it? I said I dreamt you make it to the city earlier than you thought you would. This is it Sam," Isis said with glee.

The thoughts weighed down on my shoulders. It felt like a pile of bricks. Or worse than bricks. It felt like Isis. It felt like her flesh and blood and tears were clawing onto my torso, trying desperately to hang on—desperately trying not to fall.

"Where do you end up in your dream? I don't remember that part," I asked.

"I don't know. It's not the mountains, remember? But it doesn't matter. I really can see the future, Sam. And this is it for us. Come on what do you say?" she asked.

Looking back, I still don't know why I nodded my head and said yes to her. Maybe it was because somewhere deep down I wanted out almost as badly as Isis. A big part of me wanted to escape my parents and never see either one of them again. Or maybe it was because I wanted to save Isis and getting her as far away from that house was the only way that felt possible anymore. Or maybe there was a more selfish reason. Maybe I just wanted my parents to suffer like I'd suffered. Maybe I just wanted them to hurt. Maybe it was because I was always used to Isis leading that this didn't seem too different to me.

"It's like that poem you always talk about," Isis started. "We're taking the road less traveled."

No, I don't remember exactly what made me say yes, but I remember what made me stick to that decision. It was the smile on Isis' face when I told her we'd need a good plan.

73

# Love

From the moment Isis snuck in my bedroom through my window the first night, I'd only seen a look of discontent upon her face—if not a shallow smile that wasn't fooling anyone. Even the moment I agreed to form a plan with her to escape this unfortunate place we called home, she only sported a smile of relief but also accompanied by awful fear. When Cory, however, walked into The Burger Bash, smiled in our direction and immediately approached Isis, I saw a smile arise on her face that looked not only full of contentment but bliss.

"Hey," he said smiling at Isis. I'd never noticed it before at school in the crowded hallways of a hundred smelly, obnoxious classmates, but Cory was very handsome. I could see why he had the boldness to seek out Isis. And in turn I can see how out of all the guys who wanted her attention, she only seemed to give any to Cory.

"Hi," she said back nonchalantly. True, she'd been more distant since her abuse began, but there was a part of Isis that hadn't changed, yet. A sliver of herself—her true self—that was alive and strong enough to slip out in her voice and in her smile. That sliver of herself was brought out by Cory. It was sad and beautiful.

"We're just about to eat. Why don't you join us?" I asked quickly.

"Thanks, Sam," he said as he took a seat beside Isis. She shot a quick look toward me that seemed unwarranted for the situation, but I ignored her subtle hints of negativity.

"What are you two lovely gals up to this fine summer day?" Cory asked.

I almost laughed at his corny demeanor. He seemed more immature now than I remembered him. Then again I hadn't remembered a time lately when anything felt fun, or relaxed—save for my time with DJ

"Nothing," I said.

"Of course nothing. That's why we're in this dump," Isis teased.

Cory laughed. "We should change that. Hey—I think that cousin of yours is throwing another party this weekend."

His unbearable attempt to be coy was embarrassing. I would've laughed had I not felt so uneasy.

"I think we're passed the party phase, Cory," Isis said with ease.

It was strange seeing her suddenly so confident—so comfortable. She was beginning to act like her old self again. I hoped, briefly, that eventually she'd change her mind about running away.

"But we should get some people together to hang out," she added. I looked to her—surprised.

"Oh, yeah, okay. Yeah, we totally should," Cory said, fumbling over his words like any hormone crazed teenager should. "I'll call you?"

"I'll call you," Isis said with a wink and stood up from the table.

I hadn't a clue what she was doing or why it suddenly seemed so easy for her. Maybe it was because for the first time since all this started, she felt safe now that a plan of escape was beginning to form. Or maybe it was because to Isis, she'd already escaped.


"Okay, let's go," Isis said sliding her bare feet into an old pair of faded gray tennis shoes.

"Let's go where?" I asked.

She pulled a black sweater, bleached from years of being washed over her head. Her ponytail bobbed as it passed through the sweater's opening. She smiled almost mischievously—like the night of the party. "We're going to meet Cory," she said.

My stomach turned uncomfortably. "Cory?"

"And Colin. And Guy, too, I think."

"Are you kidding me?" I asked. My eyes felt like they were popping from my skull.

"I know what you're thinking," Isis said in a smooth voice.

"Yeah, that you couldn't have picked a worse group of guys to hang out with?" I scoffed.

"Listen to me. This is all a part of the plan," she said, nodding as if the gesture reassured me. "I know what happened at the party and I know that Guy is a sleaze ball and I know that Colin isn't too far behind him. Trust me, Sam. This knowledge makes this plan perfect," she said.

"When you say 'the plan' do you mean 'the plan?'" I asked, hesitantly.

Isis laughed and pulled her hair through the sweater collar. "Call it Phase One of the plan."


The plan, or what little of it Isis felt like sharing, didn't make sense to me. As we walked through the tall grass, where I had been just a few short days ago with DJ, Isis informed me that we were meeting Cory, Guy, and Colin at the dock by the lake.

"Why?" I asked as I scratched away at my shins when the prickly grass victimized them.

"If I told you—you'd fight me on it," she said with a sigh.

Of course her ambiguity didn't make me feel any better about the situation. Despite her plan I didn't want to see Guy or Colin. I'd successfully avoided them in the last remaining days of the school year and now I would be spending the evening with them on a dock.

"I don't see how this is going to get us away from here," I said negatively as the lake came into view.

"Just leave that to me, okay?" Isis said—a growing annoyance rising in her voice.

The lake was beautiful that evening. The sun had just set over the mountain and the remains of the day leaked across the sky in a coat of orange. I could hear the faint noise of crickets echoing in the wilderness around us. It would have been a beautiful night if it wasn't so wrong. Moments later, just after Isis and I had arrived at the dock, I could hear the faint laughter of men from down the dirt road. I looked up to see Guy leading the way as Cory and Colin strode down the path.

"I'm surprised they are even friends," I said. "After what happened at the party."

"Guys like Guy are never taken seriously," Isis muttered. "And guys like Colin and Cory are always afraid they're not."

"Well, well, well," Guy said as they approached the dock. "I gotta say I'm a little surprised you're actually here," he said with a sinister grin.

My stomach turned to even look at him. I couldn't think of many people I knew that made me physically ill, and when I saw him, I was glad to have made the decision to leave this place behind me.

"I invited you here. Why wouldn't I be?" Isis said.

"Hey. Isis," Cory said timidly.

My eyes shifted from Guy to Cory to Colin, who wouldn't look at me. I didn't blame him. If I had acted the way he did at the party, I wouldn't have the strength to look me in the eyes either. I shivered for a moment, thinking about that night. Angry feelings started to build up in me again. I looked to Isis and wished she could psychically tell me all about her plan.

"So this is really happening then?" Guy asked enthused.

"Calm down, Guy," Colin muttered.

"Yeah, we don't have to do this," Cory added.

Isis only laughed and shrugged her shoulders. "First swim of the summer. Just thought we could make it a good one," she said as she moved down the dock.

"Swim?" I questioned. My ignorance quickly turned into embarrassment as Cory and Guy shot me an uneasy look.

Guy smiled. "Little slow on the take aren't you, sweetheart?" he asked as he took off his shirt. Colin and Cory followed suit. I started to feel my skin itch and my forehead sweat.

"Isis, can I have a word with you?"

I could see her frustration through the dusky night but I didn't care. She stepped across the dock then I pulled her into a grassy area away from our company.

"What's going on?" I asked stunned.

"Skinny dipping," she said.

I grimaced. "I'm sorry…what?"

"Well not actually skinny dipping. Just down to your bra and panties," Isis explained.

I shook my head. "No can do."

"Come on, Sam," she said as she rolled her eyes.

"I'm not stripping in front of these guys," I protested.

"We don't have to swim with them. Just…okay this is the plan: Let them jump in the water. You start taking off your clothes but you probably won't have to jump in with them. Just stall. Okay?" she said.

"I don't understand."

"Just trust me."

"How can I trust you when you won't trust me enough to tell me what's going on?"

"I know it's weird, Sam. It's better this way. I promise."

"I don't want to take off anything. You of all people should understand this," I said and I knew the words would pierce. The look on Isis's face shattered any hard exterior I had left.

"I would never let anything bad happen to you, Sam. I wouldn't," she said with force.

I nodded. "I'm sorry."

"Trust me," she repeated.

I nodded again. We walked back onto the dock just as Guy, Colin, and Cory had taken off their jeans and tossed them onto the dock.

"You idiots," Isis started. "If you leave your clothes here

you're going to get them wet or worse, they'll fall into the lake."

"I don't see any towel racks around here, mom," Guy said, annoyed.

"There's a fence on the other side of the dirt road over there," Colin pointed out to a neighboring pasture.

Isis smiled. "I'll take our clothes over there." I could see her smirk in the night. She picked up the clothes and disappeared into the darkness. I stared I know for too long, into the blackness, looking for my friend. I couldn't see her and I knew that bothered me more than it should.

"Alright, Sammy," I heard Guy's voice stab in the dark. I turned around to find the three of them already in the lake wading around the dock awaiting mine and Isis's presence. "Let's see!" Guy's cackle echoed across the lake.

"What?" I said, my voice giving out halfway through the word. I walked down the dock—closer to the edge.

"Well we all stripped down for the swim. Now it's your turn, sweetheart."

I swallowed the night air. It was cool and perfect. It amazed me how the weather could contrast against a situation. I had some of my best memories in the rain. I was feeling more uncomfortable than I had in my entire life on the dock on a beautiful night. I sighed and slipped off my tennis shoes.

"Come on, don't tease us," Guy joked.

"Shut up, Guy," Colin said.

I closed my eyes and felt my toes curl against the wooden planks of the dock. I tried to imagine that I was there with DJ—just the two of us.

"Come on, Sam. Nut up." It was Guy's voice, again. Cory and Colin remained uncomfortably silent. I didn't blame them like I did Guy, but their silence was just as disrespectful. I removed my top and kept my eyes shut tight. I tried to hold onto the memory of DJ and me at the dock—when the sun was shining. When I didn't have to expose myself for some plan. I thought of when he just looked at me, not my body, but me. No one ever eyed my body like they did Isis's, but I wasn't an idiot. A female body was a female body. What did a fourteen-year-old care?

"Nice, Sam!" I heard Guy shout out. I couldn't tell if his catcall was sarcastic or not. I wore a bra, but my small cup size was hardly anything to get excited about, at least I never saw reason to get excited. "Now show us your tits."

The sentence was a cold shiver up my spine. It was vomit in my mouth and poison in my stomach. It was humiliation unlike anything I'd experienced. Despite my closed eyes, despite the darkness, I felt the cold eyes of wondering and curious boys. I felt the cold eyes of objectifying teenagers. It's natural—I told myself. But my excuses didn't stop my knees from shaking nor did it stop me from feeling like I'd just compromised my innocence for a ploy.

"Back off," Cory said. It was a small relief that only compromised the tension briefly. In fact, it only reminded me that there was more than one pair of eyes lurking at me through the shadows.

"Well are you gonna lose the shorts and join us or not, Sam?" Guy asked. He'd stop asking me to remove my bra, but I felt more trapped than ever—like a robin being targeted by a fox.

"Are you going to stand there all night and be a tease or what?" Guy continued.

I breathed heavily. I could feel my heart pound against the wall of my chest—with each thud it sounded like shards were breaking off and falling into my stomach. I slid my fingertips slowly to the waist of my jean shorts—fiddling for the button. My fingers were shaking violently. I was fortunate they couldn't see them through the darkness. Time seemed to stop. I was brave enough, if only for a moment, to open my eyes in an attempt to find the onlookers in the water. It was dark of course but I could still see them thanks to the unforgiving moon. Guy was front and center as if I were a rock star and he were my biggest fan. Colin and Cory were further away. They didn't stare like Guy. They switched from awkward glances to me and one another.

I closed my eyes again as soon as I pushed the button out of the jean loop. I grasped the zipper, and took a deep breath. Before I could muster the strength to rip the zipper down the line of metal teeth, I felt something tug at my elbow. I stumbled and turned around to find Isis grasping my shirt in her hands and motioning for her to follow her. "Come on!" she stressed in a whisper.

As she ran, I picked up my shoes and followed suit. My heart was pounding faster and harder than ever.

"Hey!" Guy yelled. "Where are y'all going?"

We ran down the dirt road. It was difficult to see but as we bypassed the fence, I didn't see the boys' clothes. "What are we doing?" I asked.

"Making bank," Isis said with a chuckle.

I pulled on my shirt as we ran down the road and around where a pickup truck was parked.

"Get in!" Isis said as she jumped in the bed of the truck.

"Who?" I asked. For a quick, scared moment, I thought DJ was driving Jonathan's truck. It wasn't. As I climbed in the back I noticed the woman in the passenger seat. "Is that Carly?" I asked.

Isis nodded. "She felt badly about what happened at her party. So I asked her if she'd pick us up and get us out of here in a hurry."

"Do they know…?" I asked as I realized I didn't even know what I was asking. Isis shook her head. "What exactly did we just do?" I asked confused.

It was at that moment that Isis held up a fat stack of money. "We started funding The Adventure that's what we did," she said.

"You stole their money?" I asked shocked.

"Absolutely."

"I can't believe you did that," I said as I moved the hair away from my mouth.

"Why not?" Isis called out over the wind in the air and the rumble of the engine.

"It's wrong," I said.

"How wrong was that party?" she asked.

"That's different."

"Is it? Because all I know is that night they did bad things. We might've done something bad tonight but it is to get us somewhere good. They just did it because…well because they're bad," she hissed.

"Guy is a tool. I'll give you that one. And maybe Colin isn't as clean as he should be…but Cory?" I questioned.

Isis looked away from me. I hesitated to continue: she had just stolen money from the one boy who seemed to like her for her and not what her body looked like.

"Why Cory, Isis?" I asked.

"Boys are boys Sam. I don't think we can trust any of them." she said.

"I think that one really liked you, though," I protested.

"Sam. You just don't know, okay?" she snapped. "Besides he had the most," she said, shaking the stack of money. "Lucky for us he's a trust fund baby," she laughed. "Wonder what that's like." I shook my head both at her curiosity and her action. I understood, though. And that's the part that perhaps bothered me the most. I justified her thievery just as easily, if not easier than I did the action of me taking off my shirt to distract a group of teenage boys.

The wind from the open summer night blew in our faces. We continuously pushed the strains of our long hair away from our lips. Despite our efforts, our hair kept attempting to cover our faces. It occurred to me as we rode down a country road in the blackness of night that the wind was literally trying to cover our faces. Maybe I thought the wind was trying to tell us to be ashamed. Maybe I thought that because I already was ashamed.

Carly and Isis's cousin dropped us off in front of our houses that night. We jumped out of the back of the truck and waved thankfully as they sped off. As we ascended the driveway to my house where I insisted Isis stayed, she turned to me fanning the wad of money. "Three hundred dollars."

"Three hundred dollars?" I asked. "How do three fourteen-year-olds have three hundred dollars between them?" I asked.

"Well Guy is sixteen," Isis shrugged.

"You know what I mean," I protested.

"Guy has a job mowing lawns and like I said, Cory's entire family is loaded."

"How much of that money was Colin's?" I asked.

"About twenty bucks. But we also got a coupon for Burger Bash," she laughed.

As we closed in on my house, Isis slowed and then stared out into the night sky.

"What is it?" I asked hesitantly.

She sighed and tucked the money into her pocket. "I don't feel like myself."

"What do you mean?" I asked as I approached her.

"You know what it means, Sam. I haven't…I'm sorry. I'm sorry I made you do that tonight. I should've figured something else out. I was just so desperate to get back at those guys and I wanted some money in the process. For us—for our ticket out," she said.

I grimaced. A large part of me wanted to stay bitter toward Isis for involving me in a plan that I wasn't aware of prior. But I couldn't help but understand her desperation. After all if stepping just outside my comfort zone meant that the violence and assault in Isis's life would come to an end, it was worth it.

"Don't worry about it," I waved off. "Come on, let's get inside. I think there's some ice cream in the fridge. If my dad hasn't mixed in it with booze yet."

"I had another dream, you know," she said. "Another dream about our future."

"Yeah?" I said entertaining my friend.

"We need the money, Sam. We're going…we'll get out of this town. We'll get away from the problems," she said with a nod that looked more like it was to reassure her than myself. I nodded back.

"Of course we will," I said with confidence.

"I love you. You know that, right?" she asked.

I smiled. "I love you, too, Isis. You're my sister."

She looked out into the trees for a moment and smiled.

"Do you want to go to the pine?" I asked.

She looked at me suspiciously. "You hate going to the pine."

"I don't hate it. I'm just not good at it. Climbing, that is. But you haven't been in such a—"

"I don't want to, Sam," she said, quickly, as she walked toward the front door.

"I think I'll just let myself in. Are you coming?" she asked.

I stared up at the sky for a moment. "In a minute. I want to look at the sky for a moment," I said.

Isis looked at me suspiciously again. "What is wrong with you, city slick?" she asked.

"I don't know. I'm just enjoying it," I said.

Isis turned back and snuck slowly and quietly into my house. I walked along the edge of the house and glared up at the moon as I thought about the night. I wondered where we would go, whenever we decided we had enough money to do it. I wondered if we'd go to the city—if Isis could be happy there. I wondered if we would go to the mountains and if I could be happy there. I stared at the sky for what felt like an hour although I knew it was only a few minutes. I knew it was longer than I'd ever really looked before.

"Nice night, isn't it?" I heard a voice that made me jump. When my heart settled, I looked through the shadows to see DJ approaching from the Cassidy house.

"DJ," I said relieved and excited. "What are you doing here?"

"I live like ten feet that way," he laughed and pointed at his house.

I laughed, too. "I mean out here tonight."

"Same as you I guess. Looking at the stars," he said. "I just finished up working on my car when it got dark. Just didn't feel like going back inside. Not while….you know, Elliot is there."

My smile faded. The name and thought of the man's face sent awful shivers up my spine. It made me sick to my stomach.

"I understand," I said. "Isis is sleeping over at my house. You know…to…" my voice trailed off.

"Oh, so that's where she is," DJ said shrugging. "I wondered."

"She just feels safer," I said, hesitantly.

DJ looked down. "I hate that I can't protect her," he muttered.

"Oh, no, no. DJ I don't—"I started but he stopped me.

"I know what you meant. I just mean...after mom passed. I don't know. We have dad but...Isis feels like my responsibility. I have to take care of her," DJ said. There was a silence that arose between us, but thankfully, not for long. "At least she has you," DJ as he nudged my shoulder. He stood close to me and I felt my heart begin to race once more.

"Like I said before, you're a good friend," he said.

I smiled. I knew I was blushing but I hoped the darkness of night covered it.

"You love her?" he asked. I looked at him—confused. "You love her. Like family," he said.

"I do," I said. He smiled widely and moved closer to me.

I couldn't believe what was happening. As he moved closer and rested his finger just under my chin, slowly tilting my head upward, I breathed slowly and heavily. He moved in quickly and his lips pressed against mine and we savored a lengthy kiss. My entire body and mind changed in that instant. It was my first kiss. I couldn't kid myself any longer—it was my first love. Yes, I loved Isis. I even loved my family. But DJ Cassidy—I loved him, too.

# The Road Often Traveled

DJ's bedroom wasn't anything like I imagined it. I always thought—if I ever saw the inside of his own private corner of the Cassidy house, I'd see a messy room where car magazines, clothes, and maybe empty cigarette packs lay scattered around. I imagined I'd see hotrod posters taped to the wall or maybe a supermodel in the smallest bikini fathomable on the sands of some perfect beach. I was wrong.

After our kiss—our first kiss—my first kiss, he led me secretly into his house. Admittedly I felt uneasy for two different reasons, leaving Isis alone at my house and being in a house with Elliot. My hormone raging body, however, convinced me that Isis was already half asleep in my bed and that as long as I was with DJ in his room, I didn't have to worry about anything else. I scarcely remember walking down the hall. I scarcely remember barging into his room as he continued to kiss me. Nor do I hardly remember collapsing on his bed, DJ against me as we continued to kiss all the more passionately.

At some point when we stopped long enough to see each other, to appreciate each other, I caught a small glimpse of the world inside DJ's room. It was neat—completely tidy. There was only one single poster hanging on the wall and it was of an obscure rock band I'd never heard of before. I didn't even see one hotrod—or bikini. In that moment I realized that maybe I didn't know DJ as much as I thought I did, and that feeling was a rush of pure excitement when I contemplated the fact that I was discovering someone completely astonishing who'd lived beside me for the better part of a decade.

"Are you okay?" he whispered letting go of my lips long enough to ask.

"Of course," I replied in the same volume with a smile.

And to my delight he smiled too. And the night continued just like that for what felt like minutes, but was truly hours. We kissed and kissed and kissed. To be as inexperienced as I was, he made up for with patience and understanding. Although, to be honest I never felt like I didn't know what I was doing. It was so natural—kissing him, feeling him. I didn't know if it felt so natural because this is what it was like to be intimate with another person, or if it was because DJ and I had some special bond. A click that flickered inside our hearts and burned like a fuse until it exploded onto our lips. I laughed subtly onto his bottom lip when the thought hit my mind. He smiled at my giddiness—it had to make him feel good.

At some point the room had completely darkened. The moon was hiding from his bedroom as were the stars. There was only one light that burned in the blackness of DJ's room. An old alarm clock sat unevenly on his nightstand. The green lights glowing from the digital screen hit my arm and for an instant I could see the chill bumps that I know he could feel over my body.

"Won't your dad hear?" I finally asked.

"No," DJ whispered. "He never hears. He never hears anything in this house, I mean. One time I tripped over my books and busted my head on the night stand. I yelled out every word my mother taught me not to say. He never even made a peep," DJ said with a chuckle.

I laughed too loudly and rolled over on the bed—digging my face into his pillow. I could smell him. The smell of cheap boy shampoo and motor oil.

"Hush," he shushed me through a laugh. "Don't test my theory," he said. I could hardly see his face through the darkness but I knew he was smiling just like he knew I was too.

"It's okay," I started. "I have to go anyway."

"Why?" I heard his voice change. "Stay with me."

"I can't," I said disappointedly. "Isis is at my house…" My voice trailed off. It was now that I realized I had abandoned my friend to indulge in self pleasures. The thought of her wondering where I was and if I were okay haunted me. I wanted to vomit all over the motor-oil smelling pillows. I crawled off the bed, stumbling to find my step.

"I don't understand," I heard DJ mutter.

"Don't understand what?"

"Why is she there? With you?" DJ said.

I could hear his jealousy through the black abyss. A brother's need to protect his sister, the thought ran through my head.

"It's just…she feels better not sleeping in this house," I stated. It was then that I let my mind wander away from my evening of bliss and into the world in which I had truly found myself. "Your dad really doesn't hear anything at night…does he?" I said.

"Hey, how do you think that makes me feel?" DJ snapped.

"Oh no, I'm sorry, DJ, I'm sorry. It's just…I don't know. You didn't know. You didn't know any of this until the police came," I said grabbing onto his arm. He was silent for several minutes. I waited. I could only hear my own breath and the ticking sound of that unsettling alarm clock. The green light seemed to burst through the room now, forcing itself into the room's darkness.

"I need to get him out of this house," DJ said, finally.

I reached, tracing my fingertips along the skin of his forearm until I found his hand, which I clasped tightly in my own. I wanted to tell him, right then and there, that Isis and I had started developing plans to leave town. I wanted to tell him to pack a bag and come with us. We could take his truck or his hotrod and leave without turning back. It was a great plan, however. I knew it was unrealistic. There were only two things that did seem realistic that night as I sat on the corner of his bed: One, DJ wouldn't pack a bag and run away from his world and two, I didn't want to pack a bag and run away from him.

"Where were you?" Isis called out as I slipped through my bedroom window. I could tell by the startled sound of her voice that she'd only just woken up. I quickly stepped out of my jeans and removed my shirt and tossed the wet clothes into a dirty clothes pile that had steadily grown in one corner of my room. The rain bounced off my window as I reached for a pair of shorts and a t-shirt that lay among my floor. It was raining harder than it had in some time. The distance from the Cassidy house to my own was enough to drench me rainwater.

"I was watching the stars," I lied.

"Stars?" she replied doubtingly.

"What?" I asked accusingly.

Isis didn't reply. She just flopped back on the bed and stared at my ceiling fan which spun at a low speed and squeaked as it did so. "Just doesn't sound like something you'd do, that's all."

I wasn't sure why I was so insistent on lying to her. Maybe it was because I was a little embarrassed to talk about my first kiss—my first several kisses actually. Or maybe it was because I knew on some level it would make Isis uncomfortable to know what had just happened between her brother and me. My head spun like I was in the middle of a vivid dream—like one of Isis' dreams. This one had already come true, though. No dream was as real as those moments with him were for me.

I couldn't imagine what was going through Isis's head—seeing me come in so late. I didn't know why it bothered her so bad to think about me spending time with DJ. Perhaps it was because despite her family's best intentions, they didn't function like a family anymore. Not since Isis's mother passed.

She told me once, a month after her mother died, Jonathan had completely changed. Her father used to cook elaborate meals, play music, and involve his kids in weekend projects. After Clair, Isis's mother, passed, all of that stopped. DJ took it just as hard, if not harder, than Jonathan and Isis, believe it or not. DJ missed his mother so much that for nearly a year he went to stay with a cousin in the city—because he couldn't look at the house anymore.

I knew from the bottom of my heart that Isis's motive for leaving everything behind was because there was a monster in the spare bedroom of her father's house and sometimes slaying the dragon isn't an option—sometimes you can only run. However, I also knew that part of her was ready to leave her father and brother behind. Isis never had the chance to leave the house. She never had a break.

I jumped on the edge of the bed. It was almost two in the morning, but I was wide awake. I couldn't stop thinking about DJ. His lips still felt like they were on mine—I could taste them.

"What?" I asked when I saw Isis look up and stare at me. She didn't reply. She simply shrugged and lied back down, returning her gaze to the ceiling fan.

"What's that poem you're always talking about?" she finally asked after a few seconds of watching the shaky fan blades circle.

"You're going to have to be more specific," I said with a snort. "English is my favorite subject. I've talked about more than one poem."

"No, the poem you always talk about…the one you talked about the other day," she explained.

"Oh," I started, energetically. It was rare that Isis spoke about literature of any kind and I wasn't entirely certain she listened when I spoke about it. "'The Road Not Taken' by Robert Frost."

"That's it," she said.

"What about it?"

"I don't know. I've just been thinking about it. How it applies to us," she stated.

"'Two roads diverge in the wood, and I—I took the road

less traveled by. And that has made all the difference,'" I quoted.

"You're such a nerd, Sam," Isis giggled. So did I. "But it does, doesn't it? I mean…we have two paths in front of us. The path to stay here and be miserable. Or we can take the road less traveled. The one that leads us out of this dump and to a better place. Frost did it. We'll do it," she said.

I contemplated the poem and Isis's words. It made me wonder if it was just a poem to Frost, or if there was any true life experience fumbled into the work. Either way, Isis was right. There were two paths before us, and I hesitated to take either.

"Sam!" I heard my name in a booming voice from outside of my room. My dad's voice carried, and although I'd heard it that deep and that loud before, I'd never heard it so angry. Not even when he yelled at my mother. My heart jumped as did I from the bed.

"What's going on?" Isis asked, panicked.

I shook my head as I darted from the bed. Out from my room, I saw my father stand on the other side of the living room near the kitchen. He looked as he always did, wearing a white wife beater shirt and dirty jeans. His hair was disheveled, flattened on one side where he'd obviously been napping. His cheeks were red and I smelled the alcohol from across the room. Yes, my father appeared as he almost always does every time I saw him—save for his eyes. His eyes were burning—red. They were wide and glaring and they didn't blink. They didn't dare blink.

"What's wrong?" I asked, hesitantly. I'd seen him angry at my mother. He'd nearly beaten her to death in front of me. And the man was perfect at ignoring my entire existence, and when he did notice me, it was never as a father notices a daughter, but, instead, how one stranger notices another. I'd never honestly seen how or felt that I deserved the anger in which was being directed toward me as I watched from across the room.

"What's wrong?" I repeated.

"Where have you been?" His voice was raspy and thick—a mixture of liquor and groggy consciousness. "Where have you been?"

"What do you mean?" I asked, surprised.

"It's two in the morning," he spat out. I could literally see the saliva laced alcohol spew from between his yellowed teeth.

"So?" I questioned, doing everything I could to suppress the smile that eagerly wished to creep upon my face.

"So?" he mocked. "So you're thirteen—"

"—Fourteen," I corrected.

"You're a teenager, Sam. You're a baby. You can't just stay out all night," he demanded.

I felt my ears burn. "Because you've always been so interested in what time I get home and what condition I'm in when I get here," I replied.

"What are you doing out so late?" he questioned.

"What does it matter? I was with friends. I'm home now. In one piece. Thanks, dad-of-the-year," I snapped.

"Two in the morning," he repeated. "Only whores stay out this late."

His words pierced through me like a knife. I couldn't breathe. I couldn't think. He'd never been cruel.

"I'm not a whore," I said, cringing as the word left my mouth.

He stumbled toward me slowly. "No? You weren't screwing around? What were you doing in the middle of the night? Reading some poetry?" He scoffed.

"I'm not a whore," I repeated, weakly.

"Well, what am I supposed to think, Sam? You're hardly ever home, anymore. You stay out late."

"That doesn't mean—"

"If it looks like a slut, and acts like a slut. Probably a slut," my dad yelled.

I could feel every hair on my arm and neck stand up. My skin itched as if hot patches bubbled beneath its surface. "Dad," my voice muttered.

"I'm not an idiot, Sam. I know we don't really connect—at

all. I don't understand you, though. You're a bright kid. Then, all of a sudden that neighbor girl is over here all the time. Cops are showing up talking about rape and sex," he hissed.

"Dad…" I said, as I glanced back at my bedroom door. I just hoped Isis couldn't hear him. I heard him grimace as he stumbled further through the living room.

"Oh, is that her in there? Is she here? Is the little next door neighbor lying bitc—"

"Dad!" I yelled.

He turned around glaring at me.

"Where do you get off talking to me like that?" I quizzed, harshly. "For years I pass through here with straight As in school. I come home every day after school and I go to bed early. I make my own dinner most nights. I won a writing contest last year, did you know that? Did you? Oh, wait. I forgot. You weren't sober last year—at all. And in between drinks you're too busy yelling at mom or hitting her, to notice that I clean this house. Did you know that? I clean the house at least once a week. If I didn't, we'd be living in filth. We already do half the time anyway. Because neither one of you buy cleaning supplies unless you see some on your way to the beer aisle. When was the last time I ever asked you for anything? Besides lunch money maybe, which, by the way you seldom give me. I ask nothing from you or Mom. I haven't had a new pair of shoes in three and a half years. I outgrew my sneakers a year ago. Do you know why I have shoes, Dad? It's not because of you, that's for sure. It's because that girl in there— the one you're more or less calling a slut—gave me a pair of shoes. She gave them to me. I didn't buy them. They weren't even hand-me-downs. She saved up her allowance and bought them for me. She did. Isis did. She's my friend. She loves me. You don't. So don't take notice the one time I come in late. I'm not a whore, but if I were, how would you ever know? You're not a dad. You just knocked up a woman who was too drunk to stop you."

I was just as surprised as him to hear the words pour out of my mouth in one cluster of an insult. His eyes screamed at me but his lips didn't budge. I didn't either. I felt my fingers shiver but I was too mad to back off in fear. It wasn't just being called a whore that brought this rage onward, although that would've been enough. No, it was everything I had just said to him. The years of neglect to only and suddenly be noticed on a late rainy night were enough to lose even more respect for my father— which I had thought up until this point was impossible.

He remained silent but slowly walked toward me. Suddenly my mother, confused, scared, and probably a little buzzed, emerged from their bedroom.

"Logan?" my mother questioned.

"Go back to bed, Norma," he muttered.

He approached me but said nothing. I looked up at him and glared in his eyes. In one quick disturbing swoop, his hand moved through the air and struck me across the face. The force was heavy enough to send my skinny figure to the floor.

"Logan!" I heard my mother yell. It was a curious moment, as I'd never heard my mother defend me before—not like she did that night. It was also ironic because she could take a beating but screamed at the idea of me taking one.

I lay on the floor completely able to move, just not wanting to—for fear that either one of them would see my tears. I shook. I looked up at eye level to my father's knees to see Isis in the door frame of my bedroom. She looked eager to step into the living room and into the fight. I shook my head subtly.

"I know I'm not a great father," he muttered through his teeth. "But show me some respect. Where else are you going to go?" And with that he turned on his heel, stumbled again, and walked back toward the bedroom. I stood up after I was sure the tears that left my eyes had now left my cheeks. I wiped away their trails but left the blood that oozed from my lip. As I steadied my feet, I noticed my mother still standing outside her bedroom. She cried violently but didn't move. She didn't comfort me. She didn't even speak. I knew in that moment she wasn't crying for me. She was crying for herself.

I ignored her and returned to my bedroom. Isis stood by the door. Her eyes were big but they were understanding. I said nothing and neither did she. Instead, Isis just wrapped her arms around me and hugged me tight. Perhaps I did want to leave this place behind. Perhaps I was ready for an adventure with Isis. DJ would understand—at least that's what I told myself.

"It's just a bed, Isis," DJ said, as he climbed into the back of his pick-up truck. We were out in the country somewhere off route 49, which meant we weren't anywhere near home. The sun was just going down. I could see it in the distance, reflecting off the metal statues of the city skyline. It was always there—the city skyline. It was always there just out of reach.

"It's the bed of your truck," I hissed.

DJ rolled his eyes and sighed. "I forget how much of a city girl you are without ever having the city part." He slid open the back glass window of the truck's cab and slid his arm down the back truck panel and the truck's bench seats. He withdrew an old blue blanket, which he spread out on top of the truck's bed. "There, happy?" he teased.

I smiled. "Yes," I replied, sarcastically.

"Good, now shut up," he joked. He lied down on his back and put his hands behind his head as he glared up at the sky. Even there in the bed of the truck, looking as cozy as one could look in the bed of a pick-up truck, DJ looked tense. He looked stressed. He always looked this way to me. I started to think maybe it wasn't him at all. I lay down beside him, mimicking his actions. Above us in the vast blue canvas of the sky there were no clouds and the sun's disappearance hadn't quite yet warranted stars, but, instead, a streak of pink entertained me for about a minute before I turned my head toward DJ

"What are we doing here?" I asked.

I didn't mind laying there admiring God's creation. I loved it actually. I planned all along that one day, when I was city rooted, I would take Isis to the tallest skyscraper in the city. There, I would make her climb the stairs and when we no longer had breath in our bodies, we would have reached the top. Where we would gaze out among the skyline. And there, beneath God's sun and atop man's statue, I'd show her how dazzling it would be compared to her pine tree.

But laying in the bed of Jonathan's truck with DJ, I was left wondering how often one could look at the sky before feeling too small to continue the gaze. It had been two weeks since DJ and I had our first kiss, and every moment we'd spent together since had consisted of us rushing off into some secluded part of town to have privacy where no would know.

"What do you mean?" he asked intently, but his eyes didn't leave the focus of the sky.

"I mean—why are we here? I mean I get that we are gonna look at the stars. That's great and romantic. And I appreciate that, I guess. But I mean…" I hesitated.

"What?" He asked.

"I—we—aren't we being kind of sneaky?" I asked. My words bounced off each other like a tumbled mess.

DJ took his eyes off of the great sky above long enough to glance at me, as if he had to verify if I were being serious or not. "Sneaky?"

"I mean, aren't we being kind of sneaky?"

"We're not robbing a bank," DJ said, as if this were an argument winner.

I sighed. "Have you told Isis about us?" I asked. It was a pointless question. I knew he hadn't. If he had I would've heard from Isis about it by now. She would've asked me a thousand questions…or yelled at me. Or dramatically ended our friendship because she wouldn't want me spending time with any Cassidy that wasn't herself.

"No," he replied back, almost as quickly as I asked the question. "Why? Have you?"

I shook my head. "No."

"Do you think she'd be mad?" he asked.

I shrugged. "I don't know," I lied.

"I think she'd be mad," he said.

Of course, I agreed with him. But I was too curious to leave it alone. "Why?"

"I don't know—girls are weird, no offense. She's like—I don't know. Isn't it like an unspoken rule between friends that you don't hook up with their siblings or whatever?" he said, half-heartedly.

"I suppose," I said, bitterly. It was easy to be bitter. I'd never felt this way about a boy before. Suddenly he was becoming just as important to me as Isis. The thought scared me. Isis, who had been my best friends for years without fault was now in the contest for my attention and loyalty with her own brother. My stomach turned and suddenly I understood perfectly why she wouldn't want a relationship to develop between the two of us. Perhaps she'd seen the way I'd looked at him before or maybe she'd seen the way he looked, too. Maybe she had a dream about it and saw the future, as she would say. Maybe that's why she was so against it. Because she knew it was going to happen anyway.

"I can't lie to Isis," I said firmly, "not anymore."

DJ didn't respond. Instead, he kept staring up at the sky. Several minutes passed before either of us said anything. I was beginning to think he didn't hear me. Or maybe he heard me but was too upset to respond. His facial expression hadn't changed. He glared upward blankly. His body was beside mine but his mind was far away—somewhere above the clouds.

I thought of Isis and the unfairness that had settled in this situation. She'd been too busy ever since that night at the dock to pull more grey area offenses in order to fund our trip. Colin, Guy, and Cory had stopped by Isis's house the next day looking for their wallets. DJ ran them off and when they came knocking on my parent's door, a few drunken slurs and a few smashed beer bottles later taught those boys to never come back to our neighborhood again.

Despite my relief, even if it was my father improvising, I knew we were the bad guys in this situation. Anytime I contemplated the idea of coming clean, however, I remembered what kind of jeopardy Isis had found herself in, and at the time it justified the heinous act of thievery.

She'd spent the next several days pick pocketing strangers

and even people we knew very well. In fact when Mrs. Oates called to check on Isis, because it was summer and they had no way of seeing each other on school grounds, Isis invited her to eat lunch one Saturday afternoon. While I was at the lake alone with DJ, Isis was at dinner with her school counselor, waiting anxiously for her to go to the bathroom so she could dig through her purse.

I had to admit Isis's dedication had brought us a lot more money that I'd thought we would ever be able to acquire so quickly. It was obvious, however, that her winning streak would soon be over and we both agreed leaving sooner rather than later was a better idea.

"Have you ever loved anyone that's died?" he asked finally, breaking the silence.

The question took me off guard. "No. Well, yes. Yes," I stuttered. "My grandmother died when I was four. I don't really remember her very well, though," I admitted.

DJ sighed. "No offense, but that doesn't really count."

"Why not?"

"Because you don't remember her."

"I remember some things."

"Did you cry?"

"What do you mean, did I cry?"

"Did you cry when you found out she was gone? Did you cry at her funeral?" he asked quickly.

"No...I—I was four," I said.

"It doesn't really count. I mean, I'm sorry. I know you probably loved your grandma and everything. But...but it doesn't mean something unless you cry," he said.

"That's not true," I protested. "Just because you don't shed tears, doesn't mean you don't mourn."

"Crying is more than tears," he said subtly.

I thought about his words for a moment. They didn't make sense to me that day in the bed of his father's truck. And they wouldn't for quite some time.

"I miss her," he muttered.

"Your mother," I said, trying to make it sound like a

statement instead of a question.

He nodded his head. "She was the foundation of our family, you know? She kept me in line. She gave Isis the attention she deserved. And she loved my dad like no one else ever could."

"She was a good woman," I added, clinching my arms around his arm.

"I look at Isis and all I see is mom. They look so much alike. The green eyes, the hair, the smile. They have the same laugh, too," DJ said.

It was the most I'd ever heard him speak about his mother and I never heard him mention her after that day. I watched him and suddenly it was so obvious that he hated being alone. I grimaced when I thought about how I would be leaving him one day soon, too. I only hoped he would understand when he found out Isis and I had fled, that we needed a better life—that Isis needed a better life.

"There!" he said as he pointed into the sky.

I tore my gaze off of him and into the sky. The pink strip had faded to purple and beyond the sky, I could see a star appear—then another and another.

"This is my favorite part about the stars," he said. "Before they all come out to play. Before the sky is covered in them. I like them the best when the sun hasn't faded completely and one or two stars poke through the sky and it all seems really quiet and peaceful."

It was that moment where DJ enchanted me with the way he sees the sky that I realized a horrible truth. Isis needed a better life—but I didn't. Isis couldn't live with the abuse she received at her home, but I could withstand the abuse that I received at mine. If it meant a hundred more nights of gazing at the stars in the back of a pick-up truck I could almost withstand anything.

I curled up to him and laid my head on his chest. "I'm not going anywhere," I muttered. I know he didn't know what I really meant, but I didn't care. I said it out loud and that meant it was true—at least it did for me.

There's a funny thing about that Robert Frost poem.

Everyone assumes that the ending, when the narrator tells the reader that taking the road less traveled made all the difference, means the narrator achieved something magnificent and grand. As I laid there and watched the stars arrive, I thought about how untrue that might be. What if taking the road less traveled made a difference in all the worst ways possible? What if taking the road often traveled, where thousands, millions of footprints had already been made life easier—better?

It seemed cowardly but it also seemed honest. The road less traveled would be to leave all of this behind. To leave love behind. And that's why it's the road less traveled.

# Soldier

There's an expression I'd always heard but never quite understood: You can't have your cake and eat it, too. Of course, at the ripe age of fourteen, this didn't make any sense to me. To eat a cake would certainly mean to have it, right? But I always knew what it was supposed to mean: Not having to make a choice between two things in which you desire. And that was certainly the case for me. As DJ drove us back into town, away from route 49 and all the stars you could see from there, I pondered about my predicament: wanting my cake and eating it, too.

"Do you talk to Isis?" I asked eyeing DJ

He was clearly taken aback by the question. "Of course I do—she's my sister."

"I mean really talk to her," I said ambiguously.

"What are you getting at, Sam?" he asked.

I hesitated. I couldn't tell him about our plan to leave, and talking to him about his sister's abuse upset him so greatly that I didn't want to infringe the subject upon him. I hadn't a choice, though. This wasn't a situation where I could have my cake and eat it, too.

"I mean…with what happened to her and everything," I

said half regrettably.

"Oh," he said, coldly, followed by swift silence that lasted a minute too long. "I don't know how to talk about stuff like that Sam," he said, shamefully.

I nodded. I understood. I had to understand. "She's really hurting. That's why she doesn't stay at home anymore."

DJ shifted his gaze to me quickly. "She's afraid of our house?"

"It's not…that," I said, half lying. "It's just…"

"Did she say it was Elliot, Sam?" he asked.

I nodded, thinking back to when she could scarcely get the words out that day in the wood.

DJ sighed. "She said Elliot? Why can't dad and I protect her?" he said, squeezing the steering wheel tightly.

"You can't watch her around the clock in that house, DJ. She just feels better with…me," I said, awkwardly.

DJ didn't speak for a long time. When he did decide to speak, we were nearly home. The moon shone a lit pathway down our street, all the way up until the point where the road splits into my driveway and the Cassidy driveway.

"My mother always took care of us. I wanted to take care of Isis, too," he finally said.

I nodded, through the dark. "I know. Maybe Elliot will leave soon?" I asked.

"I doubt it," he said as he parked the truck. "His house is still being built. And he's living off of disability after his army injury. He can't afford to rent a place."

I sighed. "I wish Isis would just tell someone. Just admit it. Admit it to your dad or something. I know that would suck and all but I just…" my voice trailed off. In that moment I regrettably felt bitterness toward Isis. The thought of her choices destroying my life were piling atop of me and I couldn't withstand it. Had she'd only been honest with everyone else like she had with me, we wouldn't have to run away in the middle of the night hoping that we could get far enough away no one would ever find us. If she could only be a little braver, I wouldn't have to sacrifice her or DJ from my life.

"I wish I could just make it all go away," DJ said. "Just…just beat him," his voice murmured. "Just beat him until he can't hurt her anymore." A tear trickled down his face. I reached from him but he retracted. "The world is full of sin, Sam."

"I know," I whispered. I leaned in for him again but he barely responded. I kissed his cheek after I looked out into the night to make sure no one, most importantly Isis, saw us. She'd said she'd be gone all day with Carly and said she'd make sure she didn't come home empty handed. DJ returned the kiss and I hopped out of the truck.

"You can't hurt him, DJ. It won't…it won't make it go away," I said.

He smirked an unwilling smirk. "Are you kidding? He's a United States Marine. I couldn't hurt him if I tried."

That night, as Isis laid beside me sound asleep, proud of herself for acquiring two hundred dollars from one of Carly's friends, I laid sleepless. I curled up into a ball. My knees were pressed against my chest and my arms wrapped around my chins. I glared out of my bedroom window, peering at the stars. There were several now with a big bright moon to join them. I hated watching her take money from innocent people and I hated the idea of running away now more than ever.

It didn't seem fair and I felt nothing but guilt for feeling that way. Suddenly the entire scheme had become real to me. Suddenly Isis's rape was more real than ever. I peered over her. She looked so peaceful when she slept. It reminded me of how she used to be before. Despite her willingness to open to up to me and despite her eagerness to leave, one thing was for sure: Isis wasn't really Isis anymore. I suspected that she wouldn't be as long as she lay her head to rest on our street. As if she were like Superman and this awful, awful place we called a childhood had become her kryptonite.

"I don't know what to do," I whispered to Isis. The room was silent and my words seemed to echo. In the faint distance,

I could hear the television. It was on some sort of late night comedy show. I was almost positive my father was asleep. My mother was, too. I was the only one left alone with my thoughts. I wondered if DJ had fallen asleep yet. I wondered why Jonathan didn't seem to care that Isis had spent the entire summer sleeping in my bed. I grew angry with him. A father is supposed to protect his daughter. I always thought Jonathan was better than mine—until now.

I wondered what Elliot did now that Isis stayed away from him. I wondered if he cursed me under his breath. I wondered if he was somewhat relieved to have the temptation out of reach. I wondered if he sat up at night worried that at any moment, the police could bust down the Cassidys' door and drag him out of his bed and straight into prison. How I wished it were that simple. I wished that Isis would find the courage to confront the police. Her word would be enough to at least keep him away from her.

And then it hit me like a bolt of lightning, that all I needed was questionable evidence to get the police truly interested. I thought for a long time after that about how to acquire such evidence. It had become strikingly obvious where I was going to have to go. If I wanted to develop a clear picture—I was going to have to go somewhere dark.

I glared at the Cassidy house the next morning from my bedroom window.

"I really need to get back over to my house at some point. I'm starting to run out of clothes," Isis said as she tried to fit her more curvy body into one of my slim t-shirts. "Carly is picking me up in a couple of minutes. We're going to go to the mall. I might try to dip my hand into a few tip jars. Want to come?"

I shook my head slowly.

"No offense, Sam, but we're never going to get out of here if you don't start helping out more. I've been doing most of it because I felt badly for what you had to do that night at the dock, but I'm kinda pulling all the weight now," she said.

"I'm not very comfortable with stealing," I muttered, as I glanced at her.

She looked at me with judgmental eyes. "I don't exactly like it either, Sam. But how else are we gonna have money to get away?"

I shook my head again. "I don't know." I sighed. "How about you go with Carly and get whatever money you can...I'll go over to your house and get your stuff. Maybe I can find a few things there we can pawn off or something," I insisted.

A small smile curved upward on her face. "We're really doing this right? We're really escaping?" she said so hopefully it broke my heart.

"Yes," I said through clinched teeth. "We really are." At that moment a horn sounded from the driveway. Carly was waiting.

"Okay, you go get some stuff from my house but be careful, okay, Sam?" she said.

I nodded. "Of course." I watched her leave, and I went back to glaring at the house beside mine. The pick-up truck was gone and that meant Jonathan was probably at work. Elliot's Sedan was missing from the driveway as well. I wasn't sure where he would be, but I knew this was my window of opportunity. I had no way of knowing if DJ was home but running upon him in the house would be no struggle. I'd simply have to tell him I was there to see him and only him.

I crept across the yards as naturally as possible and climbed the back porch steps. Luckily for me, Isis's dad had been lazy about fixing the lock on the back door for years. I quietly stepped inside the house.

"Jonathan?" I called out just to be sure. "DJ?" There was no answer.

The house was calm and well kept. At a glance it looked like the perfect American family lived here. And at one time that was the case. I had always envied Isis to a degree. She had a mother who loved her, a father who adored her, a brother to watch over her, and a house that actually had food in the refrigerator. And to my knowledge no one in the Cassidy household ever drank a drop of alcohol. There was a family portrait that hung over the fireplace. Jonathan, Isis, DJ, and, of course, their mother Clair. She was a beautiful woman and to DJ's point, nearly identical to Isis. My family and I had never had a family portrait taken.

I crept through the house. The hardwood floorboards in the living room were old and cracked beneath my feet with each step. All these years running and playing in the Cassidy house, I'd never noticed it. I found the hall-way. Jonathan's bedroom was located on the other side of the living room but in the hallway, four doors remained at my choosing. The first door on the right was Isis's room. The room beside it was the bathroom. DJ's room was at the end of the hall, and Elliot's room was across from Isis's room.

I took a deep breath and grasped the door handle. A quick turn later I opened the door and stepped into the Cassidys' spare bedroom. My heart pumped far too quickly. I could scarcely breathe. The room was tidy. The bed was made without a single wrinkle or crease in the sheets. The pillows were stacked nicely, side by side, also blemish free. The room had been swept and the window had been washed. On a dresser adjacent from the bed sat a toiletry bag. The contents lay out before it. A silver razor beside a small can of shaving cream with a plain red toothbrush sat on a small hand towel. Beside the items sat an American flag, folded into three points, which sat in a glass case that matched. Atop the cased flag laid a heart shaped medal with a purple center and a long purple sash.

I approached it. I'd seen one before in a history book.

"It's a purple heart," a voice boomed behind me.

I quickly spun around. My heart rate only increased as I saw Elliot standing in the doorframe. His eyes were transfixed on me. I'd forgotten how tall he was and how muscular. He wore a tight t-shirt with a collared shirt, unbuttoned, and jeans so washed they looked bleached. I said nothing but stared—unable to feel my own knees.

"It's a medal you get in the service," he continued. I knew

he could see how anxious I was to get out of the room and away from him. His eyes gleamed but his lips stayed straight and tight. "Do you know what they mean?" he asked as he gestured toward the medal. "The purple heart medal. Do you know what it means?"

I shook my head slowly. I stayed silent.

"It means I was injured. Hurt on the field. I was shot," he explained. "The bullet hit my leg. Right above my knee," he patted the area gently. "Shame. I used to be a really good runner." He walked deeper into the room but not near me. He moved himself over toward the nightstand beside his bed, reflecting at a picture that was angled against me. "Isis isn't here right now, darling," he muttered.

I felt a chill ripple down my spine. "I'm not here to see Isis," I said, mistakenly, out loud.

"Oh," he said in a mockingly surprised voice. He turned toward me and took a seat on the edge of his bed. As he did so, I felt my chest tighten and my stomach turn. "DJ then?" he questioned. This time I didn't say anything. I debated making a break for the door. To run as fast as I could out of the room and out of that house. I had just heard him say he couldn't run anymore—perhaps that was my sign. Instead, I stood imperfectly still, scared to move, waiting to blame myself for whatever was about to happen.

"I guess we should address the elephant in the room, then?" he asked. He ran his fingers over his five o'clock shadow. I could hear his whiskers ruffing against the palm of his hand from across the bedroom. "What are you doing in here?" he questioned. Another chill escaped down my body.

I suddenly felt the conscious need to speak. I eyed the room frantically. I was still looking for something. A something that would certainly convict him of what he had done to Isis. As if by finding it now in the final hour with the rapist standing only feet in front of me, I could still bring justice to this situation. There was a sinking feeling in the pit of my stomach when I realized that no such evidence probably existed.

"You looked scared," he uttered.

I opened my mouth. I wasn't sure what to say but I was going to say something. Nothing came out though. Not a single word.

"You shouldn't be," he added. His glare was unmoving. I felt like he hadn't blinked at all throughout the entire conversation. "I think I know why you're here," he said.

"You do?" my voice choked out in a soft whisper. My heart pounded so loudly I wondered, briefly, if he could hear it.

"You're curious."

I nodded before I realized it.

"You're suspicious." He stood from the bed and slowly walked toward me. "That was quite a scene that happened the other night. The one with the police and what not," he said passively. "You and Isis caused quite a stir." He moved closer. "Saying some pretty nasty things about me."

"I'm sorry," I blurted out regrettably. I wanted to kick myself in the stomach when I said it. I hated how the words tasted coming from my mouth—bitter. My fear, however outweighed my rage.

He stopped suddenly, taken aback by my statement. A small smile crept across his face. "Thank you but I know you don't mean it." He knelt down in front of me. We were eye level now. I could scarcely look into his eyes; they were dark brown, and daunting. "And why should you? You are just looking out for your friend." Then suddenly and terrifyingly he placed his hands on my arms— gripping them tightly. I shook with fear and even let out a small squeal under my breath.

"You don't know what you're doing. And you're going to get yourself hurt. Both of you!" His words were striking and sinister. I panicked and jolted out of his grip. Without thinking or even lifting my head up enough to look him in the eye once more, I ran past him and out of the room. I didn't stop running until I was out of the house and halfway into my own. In the living room, I found my father eating a turkey sandwich and looking at me like I was insane. I breathed heavily and I knew I had tears bubbling up in my eyes.

"What happened to you?" my father said, less concerned

and more curious.

I just shook my head. I couldn't answer him but ironically it was the happiest I'd ever seen that man in my entire life. The doorbell rang and I squealed once more—but louder.

"It's just the doorbell, Sam," he said with the same distaste and annoyance in his voice.

I nodded and looked toward the door—refusing to move.

"Well, go answer it!" He barked at me as half of his turkey sandwich flew from his mouth.

I moved slowly toward the door as its bell rang again. I was afraid to see Elliot standing on the other side. I knew my father wasn't much of one but he would stop anything horrible from happening to me, right? And then I thought of Jonathan and how he was probably twice the man and father than my own and he was still letting unspeakable things happen under his own roof.

# Regret

"Hello, Sam," Mrs. Oates said, smiling down at me from my front door. I stood still with my hand placed firmly on the knob as I glared at my school counselor.

"Hi," I said, surprised to see her.

"Are you busy?" she asked in an attempt to poke her head and most importantly, her eyes, inside the living room.

"Um…I guess not," I uttered, looking passed her to the Cassidy house.

"Is your father or mother home?" she asked.

"Both," I replied.

"Who's there, Sam?" I heard my mother's screechy voice coming from the kitchen.

Mrs. Oates took the liberty to step inside, craning her neck toward the direction of my mother's voice. "My name is Jenna Oates. I'm a school counselor at Samantha's school."

My mother lazily entered the living room. Her ashtray breath whiffed through the room as she laughed. "School counselor? What on earth does Sam need a school counselor for?"

"I like to think of myself as more of a friend than a counselor," Mrs. Oates said, proudly.

I rolled my eyes.

"So, what are you doing here, then?" my mother protested.

Mrs. Oates smiled awkwardly and peered down to me. "I was in the neighborhood and haven't spoken to Sam since the school year ended. I was hoping to take her out for dinner, if the two of you weren't opposed."

My mother shrugged her shoulders and walked out of the room without a single word.

"Well, Sam?" Mrs. Oates inquired, eyeing down at me with her pearly white smile and equally white eyeballs.

"Sure," I said, uneasily. I could hardly finish a session with Mrs. Oates in school. I always felt like she meant well, but the truth of the matter is meaning well is hardly ever enough.


"I hope you like Japanese," she said as we took our seats in a semi-elegant restaurant, which had a name I couldn't pronounce. She was kind enough to take me to the city, though. And that was enough to score points with me. My entire life I'd never visited the city.

"Of course," I lied. At least, I assumed I was lying. The truth was at the age of fourteen, living with alcoholic, chain-smoking, parents, I didn't get a lot of variety when it came to cuisine. Mrs. Oates smiled plastically as she adjusted herself in the seat across from me, glaring at the menu. Moments later she ordered, spatting off words I'd never heard before. When the waitress turned to me, I sheepishly pointed at something that had the word chicken in it and hoped I liked it.

"Have you ever been here, before?" Mrs. Oates asked as the waitress collected our menus and left us alone.

"No," I replied.

"Oh, you'll love it. I'm sure of it. You'll love it."

Which, of course, I didn't. I managed to choke down most of the chicken due to the fact it was too gooey or spicy to be chicken and I picked at the tasteless rice. The gesture was more important than the food. It's not her fault I grew up with next to zero culture in my house.

"How are you, Sam?" she finally asked. I knew the questions would start coming eventually. At some point this little surprise lunch would transform. The Japanese steakhouse would no longer be but that instead—her office.

"I'm fine," I replied, perhaps too coldly.

"That's good to hear," she said without question, which was surprising to say the least. "And Isis?" Honestly, it wasn't a question I anticipated. Despite everything I'd told Ms. Oates about Isis's situation, she always seemed to be more focused on myself. I was half determined to reply with another iced fine, when I thought of Isis having to run away from home and us trying to survive amongst skyscrapers or worse, trees. And admittedly, I thought of DJ. This was my second chance to try to implement some sort of true justice into this situation—for all of us.

"Still living with a rapist," I said, more coldly than my chilly fine. It was a harsh slap in the face but it guaranteed her attention. She stopped swiveling the spoon in her cup of hot tea. Her look was blank—shocked. "Don't worry, she's staying with me most nights now," I said, trying to retract my harshness.

"Sam," she started intently. "I informed the principal. I called the police—they told me they sent an officer," she said, desperately.

I nodded my head. "I know. I know. I was there," I assured her. I could see her chest heave in a sigh of relief, which angered me. Was it enough for her that she only did her part? Not that the issue was resolved.

"They asked a question or two then left," I remarked.

She wiped the corners of her mouth with a napkin that sat in her lap. "I wasn't there, so I am not sure of the details. But from what I heard, Sam, when the police started asking questions, Isis denied any such allegations," she said, too calmly for my liking.

"She was lying," I said, firmly.

Mrs. Oates smiled at me. It wasn't the kind of smile you see when from someone when you just hit a home run or got the bonus question right on a history test. It was the kind of smile you see when you strike out. The kind of smile you see when you bring down the grading curve.

"Perhaps she was, sweetie," she said in a mockingly attentive sort of way. "But the police have questioned her twice. They've questioned her father and her brother, too. None of them reported any strange activity happening in the house. None of them suspected Mr. Kerns of anything...inappropriate," she explained.

"DJ said that?" I questioned. I was astonished before I realized that the questioning happened before I'd ever had the chance to talk to him about the situation.

"I'm not lying," I said, grasping my hands tightly around the corners of my chair. I could feel the blood pumping through my veins. If I had looked down at my hands at the moment, I'm sure I would've seen purplish digits, seemingly about to bust.

"I know you're not," Mrs. Oates said calmly, and somewhat reassuringly. You know, Sam," she started. She picked up her recently placed fortune cookie and with a quick twist of her skinny fingers, she popped the cookie in half. "It isn't uncommon for us to project some nugget of truth into a bigger untruth," she said.

"Untruth?" I questioned. "You mean a lie."

"Not exactly, Sam."

"No, that's what you mean. You think I'm lying."

"No, I don't."

"Uh, yes, you totally think I'm lying," I hissed.

Mrs. Oates sighed and she rubbed her temples. "What I mean, Sam, is that sometimes we have a difficult time facing reality. So, when we're trying to express something very true and very real in our lives but can't, we project onto something or someone else."

It took me a little over five seconds to fully realize what she was implying. And the moment I did, I felt a horrible sinking feeling from my chest down to my belly button. "You think I was raped?" I asked in a hushed whisper. She didn't reply, but

*113*

her mellow eyes and her slightly quivered lips told me yes. I looked down at the table, which was clad in a thick black and white cloth with some sort of dragon themed design. I picked at the corner of the table for a moment, doing my best to withhold tears of frustration and embarrassment. I picked up my fortune cookie, ripped it out of its plastic and broke it in half as I pretended it was Mrs. Oates's condescending smile.

"Sam," she said, as I watched the folded paper fall to the table. I just glared at it for a moment. I didn't even read it. I just watched it collapse among the cookie crumbs.

"You think I was raped," I said in a harsh tone. "I tell you that my best friend was raped. That my best friend needs help and that she can't do this on her own. I tell you that she is living with her rapist and you're surprised she doesn't come clean? She's scared. I'm angry. And she's scared."

I stood from the table, grabbed my fortune, and exited the steakhouse as quickly as I knew how.

"Sam," I heard Mrs. Oates calling behind me as I stormed out. I froze and turned around as I glared deep into her eyes.

"So, there's a nugget of truth in every lie, right? Did you also know that there is a lot more than nugget of truth in every truth? Does it ever occur to people like you, grown-up people who have real jobs and bills and problems that maybe sometimes bad things happen to us younger people? And that maybe, just maybe because we're not forty and experienced, we just don't always know how to handle it? I tell you that a girl— my best friend—is being raped continuously and you want to jump into my life and wiggle around?"

"Sam—"she started to protest but I stopped her.

"I get it. I know my home life sucks. You don't have to tell me. I have a dad who can't stop drinking and yelling and I have a mom who is just one drink away from thinking she's living on Jupiter with Johnny Carson. But if you need to hear it—no. I'm not being raped," I said on the city street, loud enough for passerby's to glance at us awkwardly.

"Sam, I can't do anything if she doesn't come forward. And say what you will about her home life but her father assured me that everything was completely normal," she said as if she actually believed it.

I snickered angrily. "So, obviously, someone is lying and you assume it's me," I said. I turned on my heel and continued down the street. I could see a bus stop nearby, and knew I could make the rest of the way home on my own.

"Sam!" She called out again—sounding like a broken record. "Sam, please don't leave like this, okay?" But I didn't respond. I didn't even turn around.

"Do you know why I've called you to my office almost every week during the past school year?" she finally called out. I stopped. I was a prisoner to my own sense of curiosity. I turned around to face her once more. "Your mother—the woman who is so drunk she's living on Jupiter, called and asked. It wasn't because anyone suspected anything. It was because your mother told us you might need it. And all year I've wrecked my mind trying to figure out why a woman, who is obviously a drunken mess, who never pays attention to her daughter, would inquire about her counseling," Mrs. Oates's eyes began to well up with tears. "And all I can think now…is because she knew something awful was happening."

I shook my head as the bus pulled up to the stop. "I'm just as lost as you are," I called out. "I didn't know my mother did that and I don't know why she did," I admitted. "It could be a myriad of reasons. It could be because she doesn't want to take the time to talk to me herself. Or maybe she doesn't want the guilty conscience of realizing she didn't raise me and tries to pawn the job off on someone else so I don't turn out as screwed up as her. I don't know—I don't pretend to know how her so-called mind works. I do know one thing, though. Whatever you're accusing my home life of being…well that's the one thing it's not. But next door not a hundred feet away from me is exactly what I'm saying it is and that's the only truth here, Mrs. Oates," I said, firmly.

I walked toward the bus, grasped the railing, and stepped onto the first step. I thought about what Mrs. Oates had said and marveled at the fact my mom ever attempted to do something decent for me whether the intentions were pure or selfish. I never really found out why my mother did that, but despite her good or bad intentions, despite Mrs. Oates's lazy intentions, I wish my mother had never made that phone call. Mrs. Oates raced behind me. "Sam!" she called out. But I didn't turn around this time and I stopped listening. I stopped listening—like Mrs. Oates had already done.

I didn't get off the bus at my usual stop, just outside the neighborhood. Instead, I got off a stop earlier in the dead center of town—near its square. The square, a title in which I never understood as a child seeing as how the area was more round than square, was filled with cute little "Ma and Pa" stores. Homemade cooking restaurants, a leather shoe store, an arcade. There was an old movie theatre that played six month old or older movies. There was a candy store on the corner of Park Row and Phillips, just down the road from that movie theatre. That was the closest store to the bus stop at which I took my exit—that's where I saw Cory.

My heart rushed for a minute as I caught myself midway through a wish that he didn't see me. He saw me. As he exited the movie theatre, he caught me, hesitating in front of Katie's Candy Emporium.

"Sam?" He asked. I'd felt like a million people had said my name that day.

"Hey, Cory," I said, sheepishly. I was thankful that he was by himself. Had Guy or Colin been with him, I would've felt instantly cornered. It was just Cory, but that alone was enough for me to shake nervously. After all the last time I saw him he was half naked and I was topless and running away with his pants and money.

He eyed me for a moment as if he expected me to jump right into an explanation. I waited for his harsh words. I half expected him to rip the tiny purse off of my shoulder and rummage through it. He wouldn't have found much, but he would've been five dollars and a stick of gum richer if he had done so. I felt a rapid apology bubbling at the tip of my tongue. I was just waiting for my jaw to allow itself to unlock—so I could vomit I'm sorry all over him.

"How's Isis?" he asked.

"What?" I said, confused.

"I said, how's Isis?" he repeated, a little less patient this time.

I smiled weakly and nodded confusingly. "She's um…she's okay."

"Good," he started mimicking my nod. "Hey, so random question—where are my pants and all my money?" he continued. I knew his silent forgiveness was too good to be true.

"Listen…" I started as if I had some sort of grand explanation hidden up my sleeve. He waited with his arms crossed, glaring at me. He didn't seem mad though. As odd as it was to determine what emotion was featuring up inside Cory, anger or bitterness didn't seem to be one of them. "I don't really know how to explain it to you. I—look. Isis…she needed money. I can't really explain why. But she needed money and she needed it quickly," I stated.

"So she takes it from me?" he asked. I stumbled over words and failed to respond quickly enough for him to listen to me. "I mean—she could've asked me for the money. I would've loaned her whatever she needed."

"That's just it, though. She won't be able to pay you back," I admitted.

Cory's stare grew harder. He refused to move from his spot on the pavement. He daren't move an inch. "I don't understand," he said.

I sighed at the thought of having to lie to him or worse, not lie to him. "I can't. I'm sorry. I can't explain it," I said, wincing at how ambiguous I was sounding—and being. I tried to move past him but he blocked my path on the sidewalk. Cory was taller than me, naturally. Almost everyone was taller than me. Isis, curves and all, was taller than me. DJ, okay, yes, he was older, but he still towered over me. Most of my other classmates were at the very least an inch taller than me. Lindsey, the school's token petite girl, still had me by two inches. And of course, Cory, lanky, handsome, stretch of a man Cory, was taller than me. My eyes were level with his blue vest and name tag that read: Cory A.

Cory had spent the majority of this summer and last summer working part time at the movie theatre. He worked more time than he had off it seemed. I remember Isis talking about it last summer when she wanted to catch him at the town's swimming pool the same time he was there, except, he was never there. I almost sighed when the thought hit me that Isis, who had just stolen a large amount of money from Cory had also admired him at a distance, secretly, for over a year.

"I need to know what's going on, Sam," Cory said. His eyes bounced back and forth from both of mine as if one might spill the beans before the other. "Come on," he nagged, "let's go talk."


I felt like I was behind enemy lines all of a sudden. I was sitting at a park bench beside a wooden playhouse meant strictly for children with my best friend's long--term crush. That's not why I felt like I was behind enemy lines. When Isis decided to go on her adventure, our adventure, I automatically assumed everyone and everything that would want us to stay here, which was everyone, were now enemies. Cory was now an enemy. And Doyle Park was enemy grounds. It was a mile away from the town swimming pool—the same one Isis would look for Cory on hot summer days. And it was unknown to most that a couple of those days she happened to spot Cory in Doyle Park, instead of the pool.

"So…this is a spot you and Isis use to hang out, right?" I asked, thinking out loud.

Cory looked like I had just uncovered his superhero alter ego. He was surprised but a little proud. "How did you know?" he asked.

I let out a quick laugh. "Cory, she's my best friend," I said.

"So, you know this is where we both had our first kiss?"

It was my turn to look surprised. I laughed but realized soon after my chuckle that he was serious. "Really?"

He nodded his head. "Over there," he gestured toward the playground beside a row of monkey bars. "Right there, I kissed her for the first time. I was so nervous," he said.

"When was this?" I asked.

He shrugged. "I don't know. Last summer?" he said.

"Hmm," I hummed. We sat in silence for a few moments. Whatever Isis and Cory were, it was obviously something more than I ever thought it to be. I smiled for a second. We were best friends, Isis and I, yet we both hid little details like our first kiss from each other. For different reasons maybe, but still...reasons.

"I don't understand what's happening," Cory said, anxiously. He looked worried. Cory Allison was the most handsome, coolest, laid-back guy at our school by a long shot. Every girl had a fantasy about Cory Allison. I even had a couple. But things like fast cars and football always seemed to be on the forefront of his maybe slightly immature mind, except for when it came to Isis Cassidy. It wasn't until that moment, as children laughed as their older siblings pushed them on the swing set and as they played pirates on the big boat shaped jungle gym, and dared one another to climb atop the monkey bars, that I realized Isis leaving town meant her leaving love—just like me.

"Cory," I said, unsure if I would be able to finish my thought. I didn't want to compromise Isis's trust or her secret, but I thought if there was anyone who would understand her pain and her emergence more than myself or her brother, it would be the only other boy who seemed to love and care for her as much as us. "There's something going on with Isis. Something you don't know about. Something you can't really know about but...well, the money," I said, breaking my sentences into the smallest bits that I could. Looking back, I realized how childish I must've sounded. I would be embarrassed if I thought for one second Cory Allison was any more of an adult than myself at the time.

"Cory, she needs the money because she has to leave," I blurted out. His eyes seemed to drop like a hawk diving toward the ground.

"What do you mean?" he snapped. I almost heard anger in the depths of his words.

I fidgeted on the park bench. "She has to go. Leave. She has to leave town for a little while, or maybe a long while, and she needs the money to do it," I explained.

"Leave?" he questioned as if he just now heard the statement.

"Yes," I replied coolly.

"Why?"

"I can't say."

"Why?"

"I just can't," I said, eager to get passed this point of the conversation.

He sighed and stood up from the bench. He removed his blue vest, to expose the white colored shirt underneath. "This is crap, Sam," he spat out. I knew he wasn't as upset about losing the money as he was at the thought of losing Isis. That's what made the next sentence, unfortunately easier to say.

"You don't know what's happened, Cory. She has to get out," I said, before I realized it.

He stopped his pacing and fixated on me. His jaw muscles tightened. I could see beneath the stubble of hair that resided on the face of every sixteen year old boy who is just getting used to the idea of shaving. "What happened?" he barked. His eyes were wide. I thought about what I would feel like in his situation. If someone had told me that DJ would be leaving but wouldn't tell me why. I panicked, beginning to breathe heavily just picturing it.

"Cory," I started, already feeling the bubbling of betrayal ooze out of me. "Cory, Isis was raped." The words were out of my mouth before I could realize it. His mouth parted and he nearly collapsed onto the bench across from me.

"What?" he finally asked, in his softest whisper after several seconds of silence.

I nodded. "She was raped...more than once," I said. He looked like I had just ran over his dog.

"Who?" he asked.

I shook my head. "Just some guy who is staying with her family right now," I explained. "Cory, you can't tell anyone about this. I don't want her to go. I don't want to go either. But unless something happens between now and whenever Isis decides we have enough money, we're leaving."

He shook his head in disbelief. "Where are you going?"

"I don't know. The city. The country. We'll go somewhere. Cory, I don't want to do this anymore than you want to see her go. I have reasons to stay here, too," I said, painfully. "But I'm running out of ideas...You have to help me," I pleaded. It was an uneasy plan, enlisting Cory for help; it wasn't an idea I was planning to take, either. I couldn't, however, help it that I wanted to be happy. And I wanted Isis to be happy, too.

"You gotta call the cops," he said, as if it were that simple.

I shook my head. "We've tried that. And I tried telling an adult—multiple adults actually. I even snuck into the guy's room to look for evidence. I didn't find any—obviously. And I got out of there just in the nick of time. I'm running out of ideas," I said, desperately.

Cory Allison thought harder than I'd ever seen him think and after several minutes of him staring at the tips of his Nike runners, the only boy Isis Cassidy ever loved stood up without so much as a goodbye, turned around, and darted off in the opposite direction.

I decided to catch a bus to the next stop, which would be just beside my street. As I walked down that road, the one Isis and I usually walked together, I regretted ever saying anything to Cory. In fact, I had regretted ever feeling like it was my place to change the only plan that made Isis feel safe, just because I was in the beginnings of my first summer love. It was captivating, that love, though. And my emotions to hold onto it only tripled when I realized it was something that Isis could have with Cory as well. But now that he knew her secrets, I felt a sick twist in my stomach that I had somehow ruined it for her.

It felt odd and wrong that I thought that way. After all no one should ever lose interest in their love because she or he might be a rape victim. It was, however, something that stuck out into my mind from the moment I saw Cory run away from the park. I knew I had to come clean to Isis. She would be mad, but reasonably. Soon, according to her, we would pack our bags and leave this town behind. It wouldn't matter who knew what because soon we would be somewhere else. Someone no one knew Isis or Sam and maybe finally I could change my stupid name.

My quick relief of hope dwindled when I thought of having to leave DJ. I contemplated telling Isis about that as well and asking if DJ could be the only one who knew where we were going or better yet, could come with us. It wouldn't hurt having an older male by our sides. The idea seemed perfect. As I walked up the driveway that split into the Cassidy house and my own, I hurried toward my bedroom window to peer in and hope to find Isis.

Before I could reach my window, however, I heard the screen door from the Cassidy house open so quickly I wouldn't have been surprised if it flew off the hinges. I turned around, half expecting to see DJ coming toward me or even Jonathan, or unfortunately—Elliot. Instead I saw Isis red-faced, eyebrows wrinkled, and tears bubbling up in her eyelids as she power walked straight for me. My heart sank. I wasn't here and somehow he got to her. The thought sickened me. "What happened?"

And that's when a most unexpected move by Isis occurred: I felt the quick cold sting of her open palm smack against my face. I whimpered as I recoiled and grabbed my face as I glared back at her. Her eyes were wide and white. Two small black dots raged in the center—almost vibrating. I'd never seen her so angry—ever. "What was that?" I asked, although I was almost perfectly positive I knew why my best friend had just slapped me. Somehow, someway, Cory Allison got to her before I did and now that her secret was revealed to the one boy she cared about in this "toxic dump-of-a-town-that-not-even-rats-want-to-live-in" that Isis so graciously called it, now knew what horrible happenings had gone on in the life of Isis Cassidy.

"Isis," I started before she could reply. "I'm sor—" but my preemptive apology was interrupted by a startling sentence.

"You're screwing my brother," she said, coldly and bitterly.

"What?" I couldn't hardly believe her despite the fact she was two feet from me practically yelling in my face. "I'm not screwing anyone," I reacted.

"Don't lie to me, Samantha," she said, and I suddenly felt like we were strangers. She'd never used my actual name—not even once. "I heard DJ talking to one of his buddies on the phone. I went over there this morning, you know, to let my dad think I had actually spent a night in the house. I was being careful so DJ didn't hear me when I crept out of my room with a bag of clothes. He was sitting there talking to Tommy. Said he had been seeing the 'hot neighbor girl, Sam,' behind everyone's back because no one could know what they were doing," she said through gritted teeth. "So what were you doing, Sam? If you weren't screwing him, what were you doing?"

I stuttered for a long time. I shook my head, a lot. I wasn't sleeping with DJ, but I knew this wasn't really about sex. At least, I didn't think so. It was about something else—my loyalty appeared to Isis, to be shifting. And I couldn't say I blamed her for feeling that way; I wasn't sure she was completely wrong.

"Isis," I pleaded. "We're just—we're not having sex. We're not. We're just…we are dating. Sorta. We're together," I said in chopped sentences of uncertainty. My words, despite them being true, despite leveling Isis's worst fear, didn't seem to help ease the obvious bad news I had just bestowed upon my closest friend.

"How long?" she quizzed.

"I don't know," I said in a panic.

"How long?" she repeated harsher this time.

"The night we stole the money from Cory and the guys," I confessed.

She paused for a moment and shifted her weight back and forth from one foot to the other. For a brief moment, I contemplated her being so angry that her weight shifting might start to dig two Isis feet sized holes into the concrete of my driveway. "I knew you weren't out looking at the stars," she scoffed.

"I didn't mean for it to happen," I stated.

She scoffed again, same as before. "Please. You've eyed him since you started eyeing boys," she said.

I felt my cheeks burn. She was right, but I had no idea she'd ever noticed. "It isn't a big deal, Isis," I protested lamely. I knew it was a no-good argument, but it's all I had left.

"No big deal?" she said, mimicking my idea. "It's my brother. It's my brother, Sam. We're about to leave for the biggest adventure of our lives; you can't just start something with my brother. He is my brother," she said. Her words sounded so distasteful.

"I'm still committed to the adventure," I said half-heartedly.

Her eyes danced around mine as she folded her arms tight across her chest. "Are you?" she said, unbelievingly. "Are you sure you wouldn't rather stay here with him? Become a loser like him? Like my dad? Like your parents?"

"Hey," I said, as if to ask her to watch her boundaries. "Come on," I said.

"Come on? Defend it, then, Sam. Defend this garbage of a town. Defend the garbage childhoods we had and defend the garbage we live with, why don't you?" she said.

"Look, I love DJ, okay?" I blurted out. She stopped. She didn't look mad anymore, but she looked awestruck. Her redness turned to paleness. "But I love you, too, Isis. And I told you I would help you get you out of that house. I'm sorry—forgive me for falling in love. I didn't mean for it to happen," I stated.

She stared at the ground for a while. I did, too. We both were wearing sandals. Mine were worn—nearly broke. Her pair was nearly brand new. I had purple nail polish on my toes—hers looked like she had just went tree climbing, which she very well could have, knowing Isis.

"He can never know what is happening, Sam," she said through tears. It wasn't until now that I noticed she was crying. "No one can know—not even him," she said.

I nodded silently. In hindsight, I should have thought harder about the next few sentences that flowed from my mouth. Actually, I should've left the conversation die right then, but of course it never happens the way it should've when talking about hindsight.

"I had lunch with Mrs. Oates, today," I admitted. Isis looked up at me. She wasn't crying anymore but tears still clinched themselves to her cheeks. "She pressed me again about my parents but all I told her was the same thing I told her the first time," I said. Isis looked away from me for a moment. It was her subtle way of letting me know she'd already given up on the help of others—or of adults.

"And, then, I ran into Cory," I admitted. She recoiled so quickly, I'm surprised I didn't hear cracks in her vertebrae. "Listen, I didn't tell him what happened, really—" I lied. "But he didn't even care about the money, Isis. He was just worried about you," I said.

Isis rolled her eyes. Maybe it wasn't just adults she'd given up on. "He really is, Isis," I said, hopefully. "And I don't know—I'm not saying I'm not willing to take this adventure with you—I am. DJ or no DJ, but the truth is I don't…I don't know that we have to, Isis."

She narrowed her eyes at me. She didn't believe me and that was completely new.

"I'm not saying he's our ticket to freedom—he's not. I'm just saying there are people out there that care and want to help and will help," I said. I could tell she wanted to argue with me. I could tell she wanted to rip everything I had just said to shreds. I know this because she gave me the exactly same look she gave Mrs. McKiney the day she told the class that our classmate Alex Gardner had moved unsuspectingly, despite the fact that his little brother was still in his fourth grade class just down the hall. It was the same look she gave her father who lied to her one Christmas Eve when she had me over for dinner because my parents forgot it was December, and found a present under the tree from Santa Claus a whopping seven hours before he was supposed to arrive. It was the same look she had given Dustin Patterson the day she wore a tank top to school and he claimed he was staring at her necklace.

She didn't argue with me, though. She just sighed and stared off into the distance. She stared past our houses and into the pines. "You know we are surrounded by bad people who do bad things," she started. "And although they do those bad things and no one else around will stand up to do something good about it, do you know what makes all this that much more awful?" she asked.

I hesitated, but finally replied. "What?"

"We've been so stupid about it all," she said, as she looked at me. And her eyes told me there were so many more things left to say. There were so many thoughts and ideas and emotions we had to work through, but a frustration had captured me and fatigue had her. She smiled, weakly, but it was a different smile—it was a lie. She walked away without another word. I didn't call out for her. I should have, but I didn't.

We all end up regretting things in life. Despite what people say, and despite the good that comes from it on occasion, it does not change that at some point, we wished we hadn't made the choices we had made. Sure, sometimes the best things come from the bad, but that never changes the failure we feel for letting the bad happen. I regretted having lunch with Mrs. Oates. I actually regretted ever going to her office in the first place. I regretted telling Cory Allison anything other than piss off. I regretted cheating on my Spanish final in the tenth grade. I regretted not speaking to my mother for an entire year before she passed away. Perhaps, however, my biggest regret was letting Isis Cassidy walk away from me that day.

# Humiliation

I woke up on a Thursday morning, unknowing to the fact that it would be one of the two worst days of my life. I knew it would be bad because it was the first morning in weeks I'd woken up alone with no Isis, or any trace of her. After she scurried away from my driveway, I eventually went looking for her. She refused to speak to me, and after a while I had no choice but to leave her bedroom door. DJ was nowhere to be found during all of this, and by the time Elliot and Jonathan came home, I wanted to be as far away as I could.

So, the next morning, that dreadful Thursday morning, I dressed and went about as if it were any other day. I went to the kitchen and rummaged through our pathetic excuse for a refrigerator and found a frozen waffle I could call my own. It was nine in the morning, so I knew I had plenty of time before my mother woke up. And I didn't even want to fathom the place I would find my father.

I ate breakfast in the living room and tried to watch television as I did so. It was one of the only times I could ever watch it in my house before my parents settled themselves in for a long night of drinking and watching game shows. I was too distracted, however, to focus on anything on cable. I kept glancing out the window beside the front door, eyeing the Cassidy house—for any sign of Isis or DJ. After all, I needed to talk to both.

After breakfast I decided to walk over to the Cassidy house. I could see DJ in the back, his head under the hood of his hotrod. I smiled as I watched him. He wore a white tank top and ripped jeans—both covered in the black smudges of oil. I whistled at him as I approached. He turned around and smiled when he realized it was me.

"Hey," he said.

"Hey," I said. My smile faded and I glanced back toward the house. I imagined Isis peeking out through the window in a fury that I was speaking to her brother. The thought made me mad. I started to wonder what exactly the issue was with me seeing her brother. Surely she loved me like a sister—she always said she had. What on earth was the problem?

"You okay?" DJ asked, who despite having his hands full with something automatics-related, still noticed my faraway stare and my anxious exterior.

"I need to talk to Isis," I said. I heard him mumble for a minute, but I was at a loss as to what he actually said. He spoke uncomfortably plain, most of the time, so I assumed whatever he said he didn't exactly intend on saying it.

"Have you seen her?" I asked.

DJ had devoted his full attention to whatever was happening underneath that hood. His words were efficient but hardly sufficient. "She stormed outta here about an hour ago. She was being unnervingly distant—typical Isis."

I wasn't sure what possessed me to ask the next question but I asked it, anyway. "Did you protect her?"

It wasn't until that moment that I felt like I had DJ's full attention. He took a minute to stop what he was doing and turned to me. He wiped his dirty hands on a rag that lay across the engine. "What?" He asked.

"It's just—she's spent every night with me. You know, to stay away from him," I said. I couldn't even stand to say his name, anymore.

"Oh," DJ said, his eyes shifting downward. "I tried. She wouldn't come near me, though. She slammed the door to her bedroom the minute she got home. Wouldn't open it for anything. She kept the lights on and her radio on all night. I heard her moving around later...it was pretty late. I don't think she ever went to sleep," he finished.

"Why not?"

"She was gone before anyone woke up this morning," he said.

"You sure he didn't—"

"Sam," DJ stopped me. "Ever since you—" he stopped for a moment. "Ever since I realized what was going on...I've watched. She's hardly home. And last night was so weird...trust me. If something happened last night, I would've known about it," he assured me.

"I guess she wouldn't let you too close. Not after what happened yesterday," I said.

There was a certain wideness in DJ's eyes that I didn't understand at the time. He looked at me, confused and concerned. "What?" he questioned, but it seemed to be only the first word of a much longer sentence.

"She found out about us. You didn't know? I figured you would've heard about it before me," I said.

"She did?" he asked, just as dumbstruck as the first time.

"She overheard you talking to someone on the phone," I stated. "So I'm the hot neighbor girl, huh?" I said, teasingly. It was amazing to me how comfortable I had become around him now. He didn't share in my joke, though. He looked back at his hotrod for a second and then back at me.

"What did she say to you?" he asked.

"Oh, she's pissed," I said. "She is really upset."

DJ stared off into the distance away from the houses—away from the pines. "This isn't good."

I frowned. "I mean, I know she's upset, but...she'll get over it, right? I mean what's the big deal?" I asked.

DJ shook his head. "She's going to call me out on my double standards. See, she always used to crush on my friends.

They were a little older, a little more…developed. A little smarter, and looked more manly than anyone she knew. And it didn't make things any better that she was also more…older looking than most people her age. So, all of my guy friends liked her, too," he said, bitterly.

"Oh," I started. "And big brother put his foot down when it came to guys?" I questioned.

DJ nodded. "Yeah, something like that. She almost started dating my friend, Quentin. I told him if he went near my sister, I'd kill him," he said, as he shook his head.

"She's gonna date, you know," I said.

DJ shook his head again. "You don't know what guys say, Sam. You just don't. My friends—as soon as Isis started growing up they said the worst things about her: Your sister has nice tits. She has a rocking body. I can't believe you get to live with that. How old is she? When is she legal? I'm gonna be your brother-in-law because I wanna nail that so bad I'll put a ring on it first." DJ tossed a tool of some sort onto the ground.

I couldn't help but feel sorry for him. He'd taken such measures to ensure his sister's safety from boys his age, yet, was unaware of the danger lurking in their own home.

"She was so embarrassed about the whole Quentin thing that when I broke it up right in front of her, she moped around the house for days." His words drifted and so did he.


I waited around for a while, hoping Isis would come back. I even ventured out into the woods to see if she was cooped up in her favorite pine. When I reached the tree, I glared at it for a moment. Just looking at the branches made me feel dizzy. "Isis?" I called. There wasn't a reply, and I saw nor heard rustling of tree branches. I assumed she wasn't there. I couldn't be completely sure, without climbing, but despite wanting to find my friend, I daren't climb that miserable pine—not when I didn't have to do so.

I wasted the rest of the day looking for her. I searched the town until I found myself back at Doyle Park. There was no sign of Isis or Cory or anyone that mattered to me. There were just children—swinging, playing, and laughing. In that moment I envied them. I was only fourteen years old and I should only be concerned with jeans that fit right and the Friday night dances. Instead, I was looking for a friend who was trying her best to survive a rape, while I was trying to do my best to survive her.

I looked across the street, adjacent to the park was where the public swimming pool was located. A tall, graying fence made it hard to see everyone who was splashing, swimming, and laying out on the warm summer day, but I recognized Cory's lanky stature near the front gate entrance. I thought there was no better time than to confront him about the conversation we'd had the day before. I hurriedly crossed the street and made my way to the front gate.

"Cory!" I yelled at his back as he walked away from the gate and toward the pool. He was joking around with another guy— I didn't know him. He turned around, and when his eyes found mine, his smile vanished.

"Sam," he said, swallowing air.

"I need to talk to you," I said, awkwardly. I was fully dressed and everyone else were scantily clad.

"I'm kinda busy right now," he said, as he gestured toward a group of guys who'd just lined up at the diving board.

"I can see that, but it won't take a second," I stated. He sighed, as if he were annoyed, or uncomfortable, but he didn't say anything, or walk away. He stood there waiting for me to speak. "You just ran off yesterday," I started. I could see him start to get more uncomfortable. "I need to know that you understand what is going on. That you understand what Isis is having to suffer through. And I need to know you'll keep it between you and me. I haven't told anyone else but you," I said.

His body language changed now. He looked alert and scared. "Why couldn't she just tell the police or something? Why couldn't she just make her dad make the creep move out or something? Why does she have to run away? That's stupid," he blabbered on.

I shook my head. "I know it's not what either one of us wants to hear, but it's what's happening. At least it was going to happen. She's so mad at me now, and I can't even find her," I said.

Cory looked back toward the pool. The group of guys had thinned and were scattered among the deep in of the pool—save for Guy. He was sitting pool side talking to a girl in a red bikini who wanted absolutely nothing to do with him. He turned his attention back to me and sighed. "I just don't understand. Running away—it won't work," he said.

I shrugged. "I don't know. But I can't do anything until I find her," I said. I could see Guy making his way back toward Cory. The girl in the red bikini had given him a final rejection and now, he was eager to put distance between him and the girl-that-shall-never-be. I suddenly felt anxious. I didn't want him anywhere near me, and I didn't want him anywhere near the conversation, either.

As Guy approached, a stream of elementary aged kids entered through the main gate, followed by several moms with metal folding chairs and balloons. The last woman to enter held a birthday cake. I made way for the birthday party-goers and then turned back to Cory one last time before Guy could interrupt us.

"Do you know where she is Cory? Have you seen her? Talked to her?" Cory shook his head, but I was too late—Guy was in earshot of the conversation. He slung his arm around Cory and smiled a smile so unbelievably fake.

"Whatcha talking about, guys?" Guy asked.

"Nothing," I mumbled as I turned to walk away. I was halfway out of the gate when his snarled voice grasped me, refusing to let go.

"Have fun spending my money, skank," he said. I tried to ignore him. Name calling was one thing, but I didn't want to have to explain to him why we stole his wallet, either. "Yeah, keep walking, skank!" His voice was so loud, I felt sorry for the mothers and children attempting to have a birthday party.

I turned on my heel and marched back up the sliver of pavement and through the gate. "Do you have something to say to me?" I asked. My ears and face burning hot.

"Nope. Just want you to know you're a whore thief and you'll get what's coming to you," he said. Cory shoved him a little. "Cut it out, Guy." The resistance only fueled Guy, though. He laughed and glanced back and forth between Cory and myself.

"I'm sorry, Cory. I'm sorry. You're right. He's right. I'm sorry, Sam. You're not a whore. You're just a thief. It's Isis that's the whore and the thief," Guy said, smirking.

"What was that?" I asked. I couldn't poke his eyeballs right out of his head.

"Well I get it—you need money. I mean it's pretty obvious your parents don't have any, Sam. But Isis—Isis is just one of those girls who doesn't just go a little bit bad—she has to go all bad, I guess. It wasn't enough she was becoming the neighborhood slut, but she had to pick pockets too, apparently," he said.

I eyed him and then Cory. "What's going on? What are you talking about? Isis is not a slut!"

"Sure," Guy said, in a mocking tone. "It's cool, Sam. Cory filled me in," he said. My eyes shifted to Cory. He was looking down and wouldn't dare look up. "He tells me our little Isis Cassidy wasn't giving any to Cory because she likes them older—much older, apparently," he laughed.

I glared at him. I felt my skin crawl. "She was raped you miserable horror of a human being," I said, in a faint whisper.

Guy only scoffed. "Once is rape, Sam. It keeps happening? It is sex. She knew what was going on, Sam. She wanted it. A girl like that hanging around someone who can't keep his hands off of her? She sticks around…maybe it's because she wants to let his hands go there," he said, with a sadistic grin curving upward on his face.

I glared at him for a moment, expecting him to suddenly change his tune. Somehow I couldn't even picture Guy being this horrible. Shock and anger suddenly overtook me. I didn't even remember deciding to do what I did next, but before I realized it, I was holding a metal folding chair still folded, that was brought in by one of the parents from the birthday party. Maybe it was a lucky shot, or maybe he just didn't expect me to actually have that much weight and strength behind it. Guy stood perfectly still smiling brightly, as I swung the chair as fast and as hard as I could right into his teeth.

There were screams and cries as Guy collided with the chair, and then fell backward into the pool. A red ooze filled the water, surrounding Guy as he surfaced, holding his face. I was almost certain that I saw a tooth floating to the bottom of the shallow end. I dropped the chair, completely in shock over what I had done. I glanced at Cory, who was in shock as well and watching Guy fumble for the ladder.

I wanted to say something cool like Now you get to be the humiliated one in the pool. But I didn't. I hurried out of the gate as quickly as I could as people started to gather around—there was no denying what I did to that awful person. Footsteps grew louder behind me. I assumed it would be a lifeguard or one of the mothers from the party, ready to scorn me for contaminating the pool and ruining everyone else's fun. Or worse—Guy, ready to punch the blood out of me for hitting him, stealing his money, but above all, making him look like a wuss in front of all of his friends.

It wasn't him, a lifeguard, or any of the angry mothers. It was Cory.

"What do you want?" I asked, in an enraged voice.

"Just talk to me," Cory said.

"I should have hit you with the chair, too," I said, continuing to walk toward Doyle Park.

He kept up with me as I sped across the street. "Sam, listen to me—I didn't want to tell him. But he saw me. He saw us talking in the park and he kept asking what happened to his money."

"So, you just told him everything?" I screamed at him.

"I'm sorry—look, I'm sorry. I was freaked out by everything. I'm sorry," he repeated himself.

I stopped in my tracks and looked at him. "How many people know?"

"What?"

"You heard me, Cory. How many people know? How many people did you tell?"

"Just Guy! I promise I just told Guy," he said, anxiously.

"And how many people did he tell?" I quizzed.

Cory grew silent. He shifted awkwardly and looked back toward the pool. "You jerks," I muttered.

"It's not like—he just—" Cory stopped himself and sighed. "He told…everyone," Cory admitted.

My heart sank. "Everyone?"

"Anyone who knew her. He's…crazy. He told everyone. Everyone's either gossiping about it or coming up with theories or trying to figure out if she was raped or just having sex or whatever. I don't know," he said, sheepishly.

"This is awful," I choked out, breathing heavily.

"She left crying," he said. If my heart had already sank, it was drowning now. I looked to him, my eyes wide and tear-filled. I could see his eyes were nearly there, too. "She came by here, earlier. She wanted to talk to me. She sounded like she was saying goodbye or something. I wanted to talk to her about what you told me. I tried to talk to her privately, but then Guy showed up and he interrupted—like he did with you. Started saying all kinds of stuff. She left. She ran away crying. I couldn't catch up to her," he admitted.

My heart pounded. I looked to the ground and felt like I might vomit all over his flimsy flip-flops. "Where?" I choked out. He pointed in a direction toward the center of town. Away from the park and further away from our neighborhood. I tried to collect my thoughts for a minute and thought that maybe she went to Carly's. I started walking again, across the parking lot in front of Doyle's Park.

"Wait!" Cory was calling from behind, again. "I can drive you," he said. I turned back to him and shook my head. "Why not?"

"Because I think you've done enough already," I stated.

"Please, Sam—I didn't mean for any of this to happen," he said.

I nodded as I wiped a tear from my face. "But it did," I said, and walked away from Cory Allison, as he stood in the parking lot of Doyle Park and cried alone.

I took a bus to Carly's place, but neither Carly nor Isis were home. I rode the bus for another forty minutes trying to think of places she might be, and finally, after feeling tired from crying and weak from not eating, I decided to go home—in defeat. I rode the bus as far as I could to my house, and got off just in front of my street. As I walked under a setting sun, I thought of everything that had happened—and everything that might happen. If Isis and I left soon, for the adventure, we would struggle beyond belief. To say how, however, would prove to be just as difficult. She couldn't handle my relationship with DJ. I would surely get in trouble, eventually, for what I did to Guy, and even if it wasn't by the law's standards, it would be by his. And the worst of it all, Isis would be pitied, or labeled as a slut.

I sighed as I thought about it all. And deep down, my selfish desires to stay here for DJ were just as strong as ever. Perhaps that was why Isis got so mad before—because she knew being with DJ might mean that any adventure I go on now might be with him—not her. All of my thoughts, jumbled and confused, ceased the minute my house came into view. I saw two cop cars, with lights flashing. The dusk of the evening brightened the blue lights that reflected off the oak tree in our front yard. In the pit of my stomach, I knew what was happening—I was in trouble for the scene I caused at the pool today.

A part of me was secretly glad. They would have to ask why I hit him and I would have to tell them the truth. And they would have to do an investigation. And that meant justice for Isis could be served without any adventure having to take place at all. I walked up the driveway, ready to face my fate. I couldn't wait to look the cop in the eye and say: Yes, of course

I hit Guy in the face with a metal folding chair. And you know what? I'd do it again right now if I could. Or: Absolutely, I hit Guy in the face with a metal folding chair and you would do it if you ever met him.

But just as I was reaching the front door, it opened, and two police officers stepped out, escorting my father who was cuffed.

"Dad?" I asked, scared. My mother stumbled out after them. She wasn't drunk—at least not anymore. She was crying. She was tugging at one of the police officer's shoulder. He asked her to step back. "Dad, what's happening?" I called out. He didn't look at me. He refused to look at me.

"Tell them the truth, Sam!" The yell was so loud and so violent, I thought it had come from my father. His lips stayed still. I turned around to see my mother, now clawing at me. She grasped my arm and tugged. "Tell them the truth, Sam! Tell them that your father never freaking raped you!" I was confused and scared—but mostly confused. My father wasn't a good father, or even a good person, really. But he was no rapist. I looked to him and the cops. One of the officers was putting my father in the back of the police car. The other was looking to me, looking for an answer.

"What's happening?" I asked.

The officer slowly approached me. "Second report about your father abusing you. We're just taking him down for questioning. We'll need to talk to you, too," he said.

"Mrs. Oates," I whispered to myself, loathing the fact that I ever spoke to that woman about anything. My mother held onto me and cried. It was the closest thing to a hug I'd received in years, and I couldn't believe how much I didn't want it.

Two hours later I arrived back home. It felt later than it was— it was only nine. I'd done my best to tell the police that it wasn't me who was being raped, but it was my neighbor and best friend and that it wasn't her father doing it—but someone else. They took the information and told me they would look into it but without Isis's cooperation, they didn't see anything happening. And it was that thought alone that infuriated me. I didn't understand why Isis couldn't talk to the cops about it.

My parents had also done a great job of blaming me for all of this and subsequently grounding me for having my father arrested for rape. As I entered my room, sleepy and upset, I found Isis, curled up in a ball, against my headboard, crying. I paused for a moment. I expected her to start yelling at me at any moment. I expected her to hate me for telling Cory—and the world. But she looked up at me, and started crying harder, and that's when I raced across my room and held her tightly.

"I'm so sorry," I said. She cried harder. I don't think she was forgiving me, but I don't think she had anywhere else to go where she could cry and be allowed to cry. I started to cry, too. And then I thought that maybe Isis couldn't survive going through all the stuff she would have to go through if this became a police investigation. And maybe she couldn't survive this town anymore, either. It was a poor way to look at it but it was the only way I could look at it and mean the sentence I said to her next.

"Okay, Isis," I said, as I pushed the wet hair off of her cheeks. "Let's go on an adventure."

# The Adventure

I awoke sometime between two and three o'clock in the morning. I usually sleep throughout the night without any trouble—this night was different. Sometime between those two early morning hours, Isis awoke in pure panic. Her squeak and gasp for breath woke me—my heart beating twice as fast.

"What? What?" I asked. For what seemed like five minutes, Isis refused to answer me. She just sat there, panting. The moon barely shot through my window and I could see the light reflecting partially off of her face. Her green eyes illuminated in the darkness. I told myself her tears were sweat. "What is it, Isis?" I repeated. She still remained silent. I sat with her for several minutes. Perhaps it was a stupid question, as the answer to her nightmares was probably the most obvious thing it could've been. I put my arm around her and squeezed her tightly but she didn't respond.

Finally, she looked to me and asked if I was okay. I nodded my head slowly. I was confused as to why she was asking that question instead of answering it.

"I saw the future," she said. And this worried me more than it ever had before—I just wasn't sure why.

"What happened?" I asked. She shook her head, and

climbed out of bed. "What are you doing?" I asked. She changed clothes in the dark, without a word. I leapt up as well. I was wearing pajama pants and an old t-shirt with faded print. I searched my messy floor for a pair of my jeans or shorts.

"No," Isis finally said. I looked up at her, confused. "Stay here," she said.

"What are you talking about?" I asked.

"I have to do something," she said. "Alone." I scoffed.

"I don't understand, Isis," I said, impatiently. When she finished dressing, she approached me.

"I have to go do something right now." she said in a whisper.

"What about the adventure? What about us?" I asked. She surveyed me for a while. I couldn't tell if she was trying to tell me something, or learn something, instead. The only thing I knew for sure: Even though I could only see her by the pale of the moonlight, Isis Cassidy looked sadder than I'd ever seen her in my entire life. She turned from me and slowly opened my bedroom window. I jumped in front of her, yanking her wrists off the seal and forcing her to look into my eyes.

"What's going on? What did you dream about, Isis? About him? Elliot? Me? Your brother and I? Isis I told you—the adventure. I'll go on the adventure," I was nearly shouting.

"You don't mean that," she said, calmly. "This isn't your adventure." I saw tears running down her face now. She didn't look mad at me. She didn't even look disappointed. She looked like she was something else. Something worse than angry or let down. She looked empty. She climbed out of my window and turned around to face me. We stared at each other through the open window.

"I'm coming with you," I said, fitting one leg outside the window. But Isis only shook her head.

"No, you're not, not yet. This isn't your adventure," she replied. I ignored her dramatic logic and shuffled myself out the window. I lost my balance and fell, hitting the grassy ground outside my house. I grunted, as I remembered that I wasn't the athletic one. I shuffled to my feet as quickly as I could and looked toward Isis. Isis, however, was no longer standing outside my window. I looked in the direction of her house. I looked in the direction of the street, I looked in the direction of the pines, but darkness crept at every angle and Isis was lost somewhere inside it.

After ten minutes of debating with myself, I went into the darkness, looking for Isis but I couldn't find her and I wasn't about to sneak into her house at three in the morning. Eventually, I gave up my pursuits and went to bed. When I awoke, I realized at once I had overslept. I had planned to only sleep a couple of hours, and then hopefully reconnect with Isis. I wasn't ready to make the adventure happen but I refused to let her go alone. When I awoke, however, the sun told me it was far past six, and when I looked at my alarm clock, which read fifteen after ten, I panicked. I dressed quickly and darted over to the Cassidy house. I banged on the door and Jonathan answered. "Well there's my daughter's keeper," he said. "You and her have spent so much time together. I almost forgot she was mine," he chuckled. I would've laughed if that joke didn't seem so true.

"Is Isis here?" I asked, hurriedly.

He watched me, confused. "She said she was going to wait up for you. After your dad being…well," he trailed off.

"My dad didn't do anything," I snapped. He nodded but I don't think he believed me.

"She said she was going to wait there for you. I tried to tell her otherwise. That she shouldn't be around—that maybe she wait until she heard from you. Give you some space," he said, trying to cover his original statement that probably would've been something along the lines of this: She shouldn't be hanging around a house where there could be a child rapist. The irony in that sentence would've been so tragic.

"She left early this morning," I said. Jonathan recoiled for a moment and then shrugged.

"You know Sam. Such a free spirit. Like her mother. She's

probably sound asleep in her room. Or out climbing those silly pine trees. You'd think she was a six-year-old boy," he said with a laugh.

I was annoyed and disappointed. Jonathan Cassidy always seemed to be the coolest dad in the world to me. He joked with his kids. He bought them whatever they needed, whatever they wanted. He bought Isis an entirely new wardrobe when she turned thirteen, and when DJ turned sixteen, he got his hotrod. He never made them come home at a certain time, just as long as it was reasonable. He never asked too many questions and he always trusted them. My parents didn't ask questions either—but not because they trusted me. Because they didn't really care.

Now, however, as I watched him give me a goofy smile, I realized how oblivious this man was and that despite his intentions, he had failed at being a father. I couldn't understand how he could smile at me, when all this evil was happening around him. The signs were there. The clues were there. The violent acts were happening under his own roof, and he didn't know it. I wanted to yell. I wanted to scream at him. But I knew that wouldn't fix anything. If Jonathan Cassidy hadn't been hit in the face by the truth yet, I doubt he would—not until Isis had left. Not until the adventure had carried her away.

"If she comes back, Mr. Cassidy, would you please tell her I'm looking for her," I said, and I stepped off the step leading to their front door.

"Hold on a second, Sam, what are you calling me Mr. Cassidy for? You know my name," he said with a smile and a hearty laugh. I turned back to him, only briefly. I said nothing. It wasn't that I didn't have the courage to speak, I just wouldn't have had the courage to stop if I had started.

I searched the town for the rest of the day, hoping that she was still somewhere within it. When I first got on the bus that stops in front of our street, I asked the bus driver. He was a sweet old man, who remembered us enough to call us by our first names whenever we would climb aboard his bus.

"Mr. Jacobsen?" I started, as I stepped onto the bus. "Have you seen Isis, today?" I asked him.

He shook his head and handed me a peppermint. "Can't say that I have, darling."

"Thanks," I said, with a fake smile across my face. At least she hadn't left town. I hardly see her walking out of it. I assumed she would ride the bus as long as she could ride it. I wandered up and down the streets, passed Doyle Park, and up by the movie theatre. I contemplated riding the bus right into the city but I knew that wasn't a place for Isis. If I were to run away and start my own adventure all by myself, I would certainly start with the city. Isis, on the other hand, required timberlines—not skylines. And when that thought hit me, I realized I was looking in the wrong area.

I caught a bus home. Mr. Jacobsen was still driving his route. I asked him if he'd seen Isis at all and he shook his head. The bus was nearly empty, so I had my pick of seats. I sat down on the bench closest to the door. I saw Mr. Jacobsen eye over at me a few times. I could tell he wanted to say something. His white, frizzy eyebrows darted up and down, as if he were frowning every few seconds. "Missing your friend?" he finally asked, his voice strong enough as a faint whisper.

"No," I lied. I don't know why I lied, but I did. I stepped off the bus, waved at Mr. Jacobsen, and walked down the street. The sun was beating down, harder, it seemed, than most days. I felt it hitting the back of my neck, surely burning a streak of scarlet across my shoulders. I thought about how much the outdoors were a struggle for me. I was clumsy. I was not athletic. I was easily winded. And above all I felt a little too much like a girl. I realized, even then, how incredibly sexist that idea sounded, but, nevertheless, it was an idea that was wedged deep in my brain somewhere, somehow, probably from my father.

I know the idea held no merit. After all Isis was the most desirable girl in our class and she was more interested in the outdoors than anyone I knew. She had a true streak of adventure flowing through her, and if I were going to catch up to her and follow her into a great unknown adventure, I would have to step up my game. As I approached my house, I decided I should change clothes if I were going to check the pines for Isis. I darted into my room as quickly as possible, kicking off my sandals and jeans, and exchanging them for shorts and tennis shoes. As I tossed my jeans on the bed, I noticed something that wasn't there before: a folded piece of paper.

Curiously, I unfolded it. Emerald ink, from a gel ink pen, sunk deep into the white texture. In small, jerky lettering, I realized it formed a poem. I knew this ink and handwriting, and after a moment I remembered that I'd seen this exact piece of paper before. It was from our English assignment in Mr. Croft's English class. The poem, however, was not my own, but Isis's. She'd been here. I thought maybe it wasn't too late to catch her after all. I raced out of my house and through the back yard as I headed straight for the tree line when I heard a voice echo from behind.

"Hey! Sam!" It was DJ's voice for sure. I turned around and found him stepping off the back porch, holding a tool box.

"I can't talk now," I said, breathlessly.

"Why not?"

I simply held up my hand and showed him the piece of paper. We met in the middle and he eyed the paper curiously. "What is it?" he asked.

"It's Isis's." It wasn't until that moment did I wonder why she left this poem for me. Was it intentional? Or did she come to my house to pack some things for the adventure and leave this behind by mistake? "I found it in my room. She had to have been there not long ago," I said. Although I had been gone all day, it hit me that she could've left the poem on my bed hours ago and I wouldn't have known. DJ scratched the back of his head.

"So, where are you going?"

"The pines," I replied.

"Why?"

As if I needed anymore reason than the fact that if Isis was going to run away, she was going to run to the mountains and not the city, I unfolded the paper and showed the poem to DJ. "Oh," he said, after glancing over it for a moment. "I'll come with you," he said. "Let me just toss the toolbox into the car." I smiled at him as he walked toward the hotrod. I was feeling positive now—more positive than I had felt since I met Mrs. Oates for lunch. I had done wrong, keeping my relationship with DJ from Isis, telling Cory what happened, even slapping Guy in the face with a folding chair. Although, I didn't mind that last one quite as much. Now, things were going to be different—I was determined. DJ and I would find her and together we would all come up with a solution that solved all of our problems.

"NO! OH ISIS NO!" The words screamed through the air, echoing again and again as they traveled into the pines, followed by a gruesome scream that turned into a wince, which turned into a cry. It was enough to make every hair on my neck and arms stand straight up. I turned around and saw DJ stumbling backward, away from his hotrod, the passenger door ajar. Every bone in my body felt like it weighed a hundred pounds. I moved as quickly as I could from my spot between suburbia and the pines.

I remember every detail of that moment. The sun beat down on DJ's hotrod, making the midnight blue tent almost look indigo. DJ was on the ground by now, his back against a tree stump. His head was in his hands but I could still see the tears and snot swim through the cracks between his fingers. The veins in his hands stood out so prominently, like tunnels of skin on his arms surfaces.

I reached him and although I needed to obviously comfort him, I was drawn to the hotrod. I rounded the passenger door and peered inside. What I saw nearly stopped my heart. All sound seemed to cease for me. I screamed. I know I screamed. I don't remember hearing it, but I remember feeling it in my throat. I remember extending my jaw so forcefully that it nearly felt like I had broken it. My throat burned. I screamed a silent scream to me alone. I forced my body into the car, into the backseat.

I wrapped my arms around Isis, who was unconscious, laying on the leather seating. Her body was cold to the touch and I knew what that meant. There would be no calling of the ambulances. There would be no screaming for help—just screaming. I held her tight in my arms, thinking that if I hugged her tight enough and cried hard enough, somehow, someway, she would come back to me.

I sat there for what seemed like hours, clutching the body of my best friend. I sobbed into her neck. DJ began breaking the hotrod with a wrench. I suddenly knew what she meant when she told me this was not my adventure. Despite how much I tried to up my game- Isis had gone on an adventure that I could not follow.

# Pieces

I stayed in my room for two days. I didn't move from beneath the covers of my bed. I had heard everything that happened from my bedroom window: police officers talking to family and neighbors, those neighbors talking amongst themselves about what a troubled girl Isis must have been. A few of them even debated if it was suicide or murder—and how the person, or Isis, did it. I couldn't sleep, but I couldn't stay awake. I floated in and out of consciousness with a sick feeling in my stomach. I had thrown up three times over the course of the first eight hours of finding Isis's body.

I locked myself inside my room—or at least I would have if my door actually locked. Despite my attempts to stay sheltered from the world, my mother, of all people, came in to check on me time and time again. She even brought me a small plate of food. "You have to eat something," she said. I could smell the booze on her breath. Still, it was the first time I could remember since I was eleven that my mother had prepared any kind of meal for me. I didn't eat it. It sat on my bedroom floor. I never even knew what it was she made me. I grew tired of the constant interruptions. I wasn't used to my parents caring about where I was or what kind of emotional state I was in at the time. I took everything off of my old desk and used every bit of pathetic muscle in my fourteen-year-old body and pushed the chunk of wood against my door, preventing anyone from walking in without knocking.

During the moments I could catch a small cat nap, I dreamed of Isis. I dreamed once that she wasn't really dead, and they were able to save her—bring her back to life or something. Another dream consisted of it all being some elaborate ruse directed by Isis so she could run away without suspicion of anyone finding her—even me. I woke up in a cold sweat. For a moment, I thought my dream was real. I thought Isis actually had found a way to fake her death so Elliot or Guy or anyone else would never be able to hurt her ever again. I knew all too soon though that it was just a dream after all.

Most of the long hours dragged on in sleepless intervals. I cried enough to soak my pillowcase. During some moments I was able to unfold the piece of paper I found on my bed just moments before I found Isis—the poem. I read it and reread it. Despite the beauty I found within the stanzas, I didn't focus on its content. Instead, I gazed at Isis's handwriting. The small, straight-lined lettering was opposite from my big, loopy letters. The emerald green ink was deep into the paper, bleeding across the crisp white surface. I could almost hear her voice then.

"Sam," she'd say. "Your letters are so big—so obnoxious."

I'd roll my eyes and tell her something like: "I don't have chicken scratch handwriting... excuse me." The conversation would most likely get passive-aggressive after that, or maybe just aggressive. We'd laugh, though. That was the thing about Isis and me: we always laughed.

The hours seemed to pass like a sentence in an asylum. I couldn't stand to leave my bed for very long and I did not dare leave my room. Instead, my mind stayed trapped in a room. Souvenirs from our friendship decorated my room. From so-called art on the walls, to clothes on my floor, there was a hint of Isis in every aspect of my life. And I wanted to rip them off the walls. And throw away the clothes. I wanted to empty my desk drawers of notes and photographs. To purge my room of the only thing that gave me joy on this street strangled my soul. I felt a heaviness in my chest that didn't budge.

Just as I felt the overwhelming sense of panic, my mother knocked on the door.

"Sam," she finally said after I didn't answer for a few moments. I still remained silent. I sat on my bed and pulled my knees up to my chest. "Samantha," her voice boomed through the door. I didn't budge. "Please open the door, honey."

"No," I protested.

"I know how much this hurts, honey. But you gotta, you know, face it."

Her words sent a shiver down my spine. It was abundantly clear in that moment she didn't care about Isis, what had happened to her, or what drove her to suicide. She was just concerned about me. A sort of fake concern you get for someone when they upset your routine. I was no longer taking care of myself, as usual, and my mother had started to stress over the thought of having to do it for me.

"Screw you," I replied.

"Samantha!"

"Stop calling me that."

"Listen! I'm sorry about Isis. It kills me, baby. It really does. But we gotta pick up the pieces and move forward, you know?" Her words sounded like an 80's sitcom. I didn't believe in picking up pieces and that's all my mother's life had turned into: picking up pieces while others broke off.

"I'm done listening, mother," I said. The sharpness in my tone was strong and I knew my mother was taken aback. She was usually too drunk to hear me.

"Baby," she said. I could hear tears now. It was impossible for me to know if they were real or fake. And quite honestly, I didn't care. "Baby, what's happened…It's terrible. It's awful. I don't want you to be like her, Sam. I don't want you to be like Isis."

Before I comprehended my reaction to her words, I had reached the desk and had already climbed over it. I didn't open the door, but instead thrust my fist against the wood.

"Go away!"

"Sam…"

"Go away!"

"This isn't good for you!"

"Go away! If I was half the person Isis was I'd be better than myself and twice as good as you'll ever be!" There was nearly a full minute of silence before I uttered: "Mom?" There wasn't a reply, though. She wasn't sighing heavily at the door. She wasn't crying outside my room. She wasn't even there. She left. I felt bad for what I'd said to her but it was the truth. Isis, even with her flaws, was one of the best people I'd ever met in my life. Had I found a way to be as strong and as confident as her, I knew my life would've been different. And I knew that if I was anything like my mother, my life would be a whole lot worse.

The guilt for unleashing such harsh truth onto my mother, however, left me feeling devastated and angry. I climbed off of the desk, angrily, and pulled out the top drawer. Without paying attention to the contents of the drawer, I tossed it across the room. I did the same with the second drawer. The brass handle stuck, and the wood squeaked upon yanking it out of the desk. A journal and an old cd player fell out—the rest of the junk was tossed across the room—along with the drawer itself.

I broke my lamp. It shattered the moment I hurled it against the inner wall of my bedroom. I could faintly hear my parents yelling from the living room. They ordered me to settle down. They commanded me to stop whatever it was that I was doing. They didn't know what I was doing, though. I didn't know what I was doing. In those moments I was simply determined that I was unleashing a monumental amount of anger that surged through me, and that it would all be over soon. In reality, I was purging the rest of my childhood out of me. There wasn't a child in Sam Clark anymore. There was something else in her instead.

When I was finished scattering the drawers and their contents across the room, I moved to the closest wall I could reach. A picture of Isis and me from our first day of first grade hung below a glittery sign that I made, which read: Best Friends Always. I ripped the photograph and the sign off the wall and tossed them both into the trash bin. Next, I ripped the calendar from my wall, followed by a painting Isis and I did the previous summer. I tossed them all as close as I could to the trash bin without proper aim.

The clothes scattered across my floor ended up with rips and holes in them from tearing and poking with whatever sharp object I could find in my room. All the breakables in my room were broken. Everything that could be ripped was ripped. I even tore into my own personal writing—the notes, the poems, the crazy stories that I concocted in my mind. I destroyed so many of them. I only spared Isis's poem. The one in the emerald green ink. I collapsed to the floor in tears. I heaved and sobbed. I cried until I was nearly dehydrated. No tears spilled from my eyes. There wasn't a shred of evidence that they were ever there.

It was around this moment that DJ knocked on my window. I knew it was him. I could hear his whimpering voice outside the glass. He was crying. I knew he wanted to check on me. I knew that even more so than that, he probably needed me. I couldn't be there for him though. I couldn't even be there for me. He knocked several times and then called out my name. I ignored it. As I heard him cry outside my house, I cried into my pillow. I wondered if I would ever be able to look at him again. I wondered if I would ever stop hurting long enough to look outside my window, at the Cassidy house—or anything else.

As I peered around my broken room, I nearly let out a laugh. I could scarcely recognize it anymore. A tear dripped off my cheek. My mother cried in the next room. She was, undoubtedly, nagging my father. I could imagine such words spewing from her vodka breath: Something's wrong with Samantha. Samantha doesn't act this way. Samantha is broken. I scoffed at my own imagination. The truth was I knew that it wasn't me. Sam didn't lash out at her parents so forcefully. Sam did not throw tantrums in her room until nothing was left in her wake.

No, this wasn't Sam and I knew that. Sam, however, always had Isis to fight her battles for her. She had a protector. She had a friend to cool her down and a friend to fire her up. Sam had Isis. I had the best friend a girl could ask for. Once upon a time Isis was my voice. And now that I had lost that, I didn't know where my voice was, or what it was. Now there was just a stillness. A silent scene of little Sam losing all the pieces that mattered.

It was a day later before I could force myself to get out of bed and stay that way. Every time I tried, Isis's face, her laugh, her scent, compromised me to the point that I retreated beneath the covers and into my own sorrows. I couldn't stand being in my room another moment, though. An entire childhood of memories—from painful ones with my parents to pleasant ones with Isis—now haunted me. My destroyed room now mocked me. Even if I wanted to, I could never rid Isis from my room. When I was certain my parents were too distracted or too drunk to notice, I slipped out the front door and did my best to ignore the Cassidy house.

Despite my eagerness to leave the house, I hadn't a clue where I was going to go. Nowhere seemed normal anymore. Nowhere seemed safe. I walked down my street slowly. The summer air was humid. It was warm but not that hot. It's the humidity, though, as they say, that will always get you. That was my only consistent thought as I walked through the neighborhood: humidity. The weather was what my brain was reduced to in the wake of the previous days. The weather, though, was exactly one of a million things that brought my mind back to my best friend. I'd always felt like a stranger in my hometown.

I was always looking for the urban way of life. I panted in the humidity. I shivered in the cool nights. I detested the mountains and hated the smell of most flowers. Isis was one with the trees, with the mountains, with nature. She was naturally a part of the wildlife in a way I knew I would never be—she was different that way. She was like a majestic bird among insects. A beautiful white heron that deserved to fly so much higher than where she laid.

My eagerness to leave my home began to fade and I drifted toward the nearest bus stop. Once I boarded the bus, I sat in the very backseat, away from anyone else. I sat on the bus for far too long as passengers came and went. Staring out the window, I hoped to get a spark of inspiration—or a spark for adventure. I cringed when I thought of not wanting to run away with Isis.

As I rode along to nowhere in particular, I remembered the first time Isis really spoke of adventure. Before our lives changed—before Elliot showed up. We were climbing the pine one day. Isis was halfway up the tree and I had just barely begun to climb. She was mouthing on and on about seeing a world we'd only ever read in books and dreamed about. She went on and on, without hardly taking a moment to pause. As if tree-climbing had become so second nature to her, she needn't even think about what she was doing.

I, on the other hand, could barely think about anything else while I fumbled my way up the branches. I remember, just as I was reaching halfway up the tree, slipping on a branch beneath my foot. The slip caused me to fall, knocking my jaw and scraping my arm and leg before I was able to grab onto a branch. Isis swooped down the tree faster than I could process what was happening. She helped me up, and together we reached the top of the pine.

"See, Sam," she said. "This is why you need me in your life. How do you expect to find adventure if you can't make it up a tree?"


The sky was beginning to grey. The sun was lowering behind the city's skyline in the distance, and heavy rain clouds looked as if they were accumulating. The city seemed appealing to me now. I pondered the idea of staying on the bus for a much longer haul and finding myself lost within the city. The thought happened upon me that perhaps running away to the city was the only way Isis's dream would come true. If there was a time to leave everything behind, it was at that moment on the bus. Perhaps I could finally seek the adventure Isis always dreamed of taking. The conception of leaving without her, however, left a hollow feeling inside me.

The bus passed the school and a disturbing twist occurred in my stomach. There hadn't been a funeral for Isis yet, but the school had prepared a candle-light vigil in her honor. I watched as cars lined up all the way to the main road, causing a traffic jam in Isis's name. Wasting little time, I got off the bus at the closest stop. But as I approached the school, I froze, buried my hands in my pockets and glared at the plain brick building in front of me. People filed in, gathering outside the high school. I noticed Colin and Cory from a distance. It made me feel sick to see them, although I knew they weren't the bad guys. I tried to move forward, but I couldn't. A few classmates eyed me as they passed by. I supposed, of all times, it would be at the vigil that they'd watch me. Sam Clark, Isis Cassidy's best friend. The grieving girl who lost her only friend in the world. And I hated the idea of anyone wasting a thought on me when what happened to Isis should be the only thing anyone thought about now.

"Sam?" I heard a voice from behind. Carly approached, trying to smile.

"What do you want?" I scoffed. It was clear Carly had been taken aback by my rudeness. She stumbled over her wording for a moment and then fell silent. Still, she did not move. "I don't think I can go in that place," she said after a few awkward seconds of silence. I just shrugged. She infuriated me. "I mean, besides the fact that I spent most of my high school days trying to get out of having to be here."

"You think this is funny?" I snapped. My face was burning red. I could feel my skin rising against the bone. Carly's half-witted smile disappeared and a paleness replaced it.

"I was just trying to…I'm sorry."

"Trying to what?"

"Trying to make—I don't know. I'm sorry, okay? I don't know."

Other students, parents, and locals bypassed us as they made their way into the school. Carly and I, however, remained on the edge of the parking lot in a tense stand-off.

"What are you even doing here?" I barked, but I could hear a crack in my voice that displayed my frailty on the subject.

She peered at me, maybe with a look of discontent, I wasn't sure. But it made me uncomfortable nevertheless. "You're not the only one who loved her."

"Just the only one that took care of her," I retorted.

"Really?" she snorted. "Because from what I hear, hooking up with her brother wasn't really taking care of her." My face glowed red for an entirely different purpose now. "It's obvious you don't like me," Carly started. "But that doesn't mean you were the only one who cared about Isis!" The shouting drew attention from the guests of the vigil. A few classmates whispered as they crept by. I wondered how many of them were mourning Isis's death and how many were gossiping about it.

"DJ has nothing to do with this, Carly," I snapped. "And even if he did, at least I wasn't pouring booze down her throat and encouraging her to party and screw her problems away!" My voice carried all the way to the vigil, but I didn't care.

"You're such a hypocrite," Carly declared. "You stand there and act like you have all the answers when it comes to Isis. Like everyone else is just stupid and you're the only one who knew her. You know what, Sam? You don't. Didn't." Her words burned.

"You really think what you did for her helped her?" I protested.

"Do you really think what you did helped her?" she replied.

"A lot better than you!"

"That's debatable."

"At least I loved her. At least she talked to me about what

was going on. It was my bed she cried in! It was me that was willing to throw away my entire life for her! Risk everything for her!" I cried. I stopped yelling as the tears came. I knew that part of what I said was a lie. But I hated the thought of someone being there for Isis when I failed. It was selfish—but true. And it was that truth that made me ache. Isis was gone, and I still worried about being the best friend.

I walked away from Carly, toward a nearby picnic table on the recreational grounds of the school. I sat down, hoping Carly would take the hint to leave me alone as I debated about whether or not I could enter that school. Carly approached anyway, and I felt my skin bubble upward in fury.

"Never heard so much out of you before," Carly said. There was skepticism lingering somewhere in her voice, but I dare say she was impressed.

"I never had so much to say until now," I said, shrugging my shoulders. I didn't look at her. I didn't want to look at her. She acknowledged my force. Perhaps I should've been this way the night of her party. Maybe if I had raised my voice to her, instead of Isis, I could've stopped that unwanted dip in the pool. Maybe I could've found out Isis's troubles just a little quicker. And maybe, just maybe, that would have been enough to make a difference.

"I'm sorry, okay?" she said. It was obvious she was angry. It took several minutes of silence and capturing subtle glances of her eyes as they also stared at the school to realize it wasn't because of me she was angry. "I never..." her voice trailed off. "I was only trying to help her. The whole time, I swear, I was only trying to help her."

A terrible sensation rushed through my body when her words finally made sense. Pain shot through my eyes as I glared at Carly. I wanted to beat information out of her. I wanted to yell and scream and throw things and cause the biggest scene I could. I wanted to fight so hard that somehow I would get Isis back. "You know?" I asked, stunned.

"Of course," Carly whispered as she slowly nodded her head. I peered down at my sneakers and watched my laces acquire drops of tears from my eyes.

"She told you…" I let the words slip out. I couldn't fathom the idea that Isis confided into Carly before she ever confided in me. Or if she had gone to Carly later, why she never told me. And above all, I couldn't understand why Carly didn't seem to help her like I at least tried to help her.

"No, Sam," Carly breathed. "Isis never told me anything. She wasn't that type, you know that—she was too closed off."

"Then, how did you know?"

Carly had a faraway stare now. She looked passed the school, I was almost sure of it. "I was abused too, once. It was once. A long time ago. But it doesn't matter if it was once, years ago or a hundred times yesterday. The feeling is still the same and it doesn't go away. You still know the feeling. More importantly, I recognized the signs. I didn't know her as well as you did, obviously. But I saw her personality drain out of her. The same way it drained from me."

My heart sank lower into my chest a bit. I tried to search for words but it was hopeless. I thought that after Isis, I would be prepared for anything of the sort. But watching Carly that bleak evening outside our high school, while classmates and teachers sang songs of comfort and spoke fondly of a girl they barely knew, I realized that I would never have words for something so terrible.

"I'm sorry," I said, and the words sounded defeated as they left my mouth. I wasn't sure if I was apologizing for her life or my actions. I think I meant it for both.

"I know I wasn't the best role model," Carly scoffed. "Underage drinking and assisting in theft and whatever else we got into together. But I knew that every moment with me was one moment less she had to spend being abused. So I did whatever I could to get her to stay with me."

I sighed and patted the bench beside me. Carly took the seat and attempted to hide the tears that I knew were swelling up in her eyes.

"I didn't know how to help her either," I admitted. Carly stopped sniffing and rubbing her eyes long enough to look in my direction. "I tried to get her to talk to the police or tell an adult. But it seemed like every time we tried those options, things just got worse. And you are right about DJ. That didn't help things either," I said, as painful as it was to admit.

"You did the best you could," Carly said.

"Sure, I can say that all I want," I started. "But it'll never change how I really feel. The truth is I didn't know how to help Isis—and that's shameful." Tears began streaming down my face. "I keep trying to fathom the pain and the devastation she felt every day, but I can't. I can't because that has never happened to me. I've never been raped," I cried, and for some reason, I suddenly felt incredibly guilty.

"You should consider yourself lucky," Carly sighed.

"I do, but…"

"But nothing."

"No, I do—but is it not disgusting?" I asked.

"What?"

"That not being assaulted is something to be considered lucky."

It was at that moment that our soaked eyes met, and we trembled in front of one another. Carly and I had come from two different sides of the same street—we just didn't know it until now. Neither one of us went to the school vigil that night. It was clear to both of us that lighting a candle wasn't going to make anything better. Despite the differences, I didn't want to be around someone who didn't know Isis. For better or worse, Carly knew the girl next door. We embraced in a hug. I still wasn't sure how I felt about her. And if I had to guess, she was not exactly sure how she felt about me either. It didn't matter though. We would be, in some way or another, bonded for life whether we wanted to be or not. We'd both lost a person who was a better part of us. So we sat there, crying on each other's shoulders as we tried to cope with the leftover pieces.

# The Room Down The Hall

It took a few days for any sort of funeral arrangements to be made for Isis. The police investigation delayed things, and finally after the Cassidy family was notified that the cause of death was an overdose of pain medication, they ruled the death as a suicide—or maybe even accidental. I knew, deep down, however, that it was not accidental. Isis wasn't the kind of person to do things by accident and even if she were, it wouldn't be something like drugs. As far as I had ever known, Isis was never about taking medicine.

The morning after the vigil, I heard my mother on the phone in the kitchen. Her booming voice carried through the house, making listening in very easy. I pressed my ear to my ajar door anyway.

"She won't come out of her room. I have no idea what is going on. She better not be on those drugs," I heard my mother say. "Isis was always a kinda crazy kid, though, wasn't she? Girl like that is bound to get herself into some kinda trouble but goodness I didn't expect it to be this—I just feel so bad for that family. They already lost Mrs. Cassidy. Now Isis. And poor Sam. She won't come out of her room. Isis was her best friend. Well, her only friend, really," my mother went on to whoever was stupid enough to listen.

I sighed and climbed back into bed for another two hours. I didn't sleep. I just stared at the ceiling, imagining everything that might've been. After my demolition of my room the previous day, and the screaming match I got into with my mother, I decided to keep my distance for as long as possible. After all, I just needed to avoid the living room long enough for her to get midday drunk and she'd forget the whole thing in no time.

I used the time to contemplate how the funeral was going to go. It was painful to think about but I needed to prepare myself for all the possibilities. Considering I was sure there wouldn't be a pool in the church, I didn't have to worry about Guy knocking me into one, or vice versa. I did have to worry about him having the audacity to show up. It wasn't that I didn't understand regret or even that I was an unforgiving person. I wasn't. But the thought of seeing Guy, or Colin, or even Cory at the funeral made me want to vomit.

I could hear them. I could see them in my head. Colin would awkwardly be there, trying to adjust his button-down shirt into his dress pants, and trying to not look foolish in the process. Cory would be devastated, but he would be silent and follow the other two around like he was a lost puppy. And Guy would be the ring leader. He might be human enough to not say anything obscene. But he would do it with his body language. He'd stare at the casket and tilt his head and feel bad for Isis.

He might even, for a split second, feel remorse for how he treated her when she was alive. But ultimately, he'd look bored and out of place. He'd find someone else from school, a pretty girl wearing a pretty dress, and try to console her in the "wake of this tragedy." I thought of all the things he might be like at the funeral and I wished there would have been a pool that I could knock him into.

After I indulged in a few self-pleasure fantasies of torturing and humiliating Guy in front of the masses, I felt a twitch of a smile pop up on my face that deflated the moment I thought of someone else who was bound to be there: Elliot. A shiver went down my spine as I thought of him. I wondered if he would wear his uniform from the service. Elliot would look so elite. There would be medals and people would whisper as they counted the stripes on his coat to determine his ranking.

There would be a moment where someone caught the eye of the Purple Heart and then there would be murmurs about what harm came to him while he defended our country. Isis's funeral would be desecrated by the rumors and the exciting talk of a military man and what had happened in his life. Her funeral would fall to the hands of the rapist that put her there. I wanted to cry when these thoughts occurred. There weren't any more tears, though.

Then I thought of DJ. Poor DJ. After Isis's death, I hadn't even spoke to him. I couldn't face him. The thought of him made me cringe with guilt. Isis's adventure was sabotaged by my relationship with him and despite the very real possibility that it might have never happened otherwise, I still felt the guilt that I let her down. And now DJ was suffering just as I was suffering and was looking for a helping hand. I thought about what he would look like at the funeral. He would be wearing his suit. The only suit he owned. A navy blue suit with a black tie because he's simple. He'd tug sheepishly at the ends of the coat sleeves because it was a little too small for him. Not enough for anyone to notice, just enough to annoy him. And he'd be red-faced and puffy-eyed. He'd try to hold back tears for the mourners—for his father. But he wouldn't be able to do it for long. He'd cry and he'd cry because he loved Isis as much as I did.

I pretended, in my head, that I would slip away from my seat and find a way to comfort him. It wouldn't be showy. It wouldn't be much. I wouldn't want people to be murmuring about me, either. No, it would be just enough. I would squeeze his hand, or rub his back gently and quickly. Or I would slip him an encouraging note. Something very dorky and Sam like. I only hoped that I wasn't the only one who would notice his devastation. I hoped that I could see past my own guilt long enough to see his devastation, too, and not get lost in my own.


A couple of hours later when I was getting dressed, my mother knocked on my door. "Sam?" her voice called much more gently than it was when she was on the phone.

"Yeah?" I said flatly. The door creaked open and she stepped inside. I didn't look at her. At best, I just acknowledged her existence.

"Isis's father called just a minute or so ago," she said. My eyes darted over to her for a moment. "He wanted to see how you were, and if you felt like coming over for a minute to talk to him," she stated.

I shook my head. "I don't really feel like it right now," I said.

"It's about the funeral, honey," my mother said in that tone that told me I didn't have much of a choice. I sighed but then nodded my head.


It took every summoning bit of strength within me to approach the Cassidy house. It wasn't as I'd once seen it. It was no longer an escape—an exciting portal into a different life, with a different family. Now it was a haunted tavern of memories and regrets. The front yard no longer reminded me of playing hide-and-go-seek as children in the summer nights, always allowing DJ to catch me. Now it was something else. I could see tire tracks from Elliot's truck. It was now a tattooed imprint of injustice.

I hesitated to knock on the door, or just turn around, go home, and retreat to my bed. Against better judgment, I knocked. "Come in," a faint voice called. Elliot's truck was not in the driveway, and this was the only reason I even contemplated actually entering the house. I turned the knob and peeked inside. The lights were off—a chill darkness covered the places that the sunlight didn't touch through the windows. I could see through the den doorway and into the kitchen. Jonathan sat at the kitchen table, shuffling through something I couldn't see from the front door.

He turned his head toward the door when he heard me enter. "Come in, Sam," he said, and returned his attention back to the table. I crept along silently and softly. As I entered the kitchen, neither of us spoke a word. We merely nodded to one another. I sat down in an adjacent seat and looked at the table's contents. Dozens of pictures lay scattered across the table. They taunted me; they tormented me. Photographs of Isis from the time she was an infant to last year's school pictures. Photographs of Isis with Jonathan, or DJ—or even me. One picture which wasn't too far away from me was of her and her mother. I picked it up for a second. They had identical smiles; identical eyes.

"Thank you for coming," Jonathan said softly. I nodded. "How are you holding up?" he asked, holding back tears. I shrugged. He nodded. "I understand," he said. "This time is not—it's not easy for anyone, is it? I know how much it must hurt for you. I know not many people loved or even knew Isis quite like you," he went on.

I nodded and tried to fake something of a smile. It didn't work. "That's why I've asked you here, Sam. I know how…daunting it is to ask this of a fourteen-year-old girl who just lost her best friend. But as I said, so few people knew Isis like you. And I can't think of anyone better to—"he stopped as if he didn't know how to finish the sentence. "I certainly wouldn't be able to do it," he said, skipping fragments, leaving me out of the loop. "Sam," he backtracked, "Would you, at the funeral, consider giving Isis's eulogy?" he asked.

I was taken aback, though, I shouldn't have been so surprised. Again, I shrugged. I couldn't imagine facing a room full of people—people who didn't listen to me or Isis while she was alive but would now that she was dead. "It would mean so much to me, to DJ…to Isis," he said in response. I sighed.

"Is he here?" The question was out of my mouth before I realized I was speaking.

"DJ is around here somewhere. He's been keeping to

himself through most of this, as I'm sure you understand," Jonathan said, and I almost heard a wince in his voice.

"No," I said, calmly. "Elliot."

Jonathan's face seemed to shrink, somehow and even turned a little green. It was no secret by this point that I had accused Elliot of raping Isis—and now that she had taken her own life, the possibility she was assaulted seemed all too real to her father. "No," he finally said. "I asked him to leave."

I nodded. I wanted to tell him that he should've done more. That he should've told the cops—or better yet he should've pressed charges when the police were beating down my door. I didn't, though. As much as I wanted justice for Isis—as much as I wanted Elliot to pay for what he did, I hadn't the energy to fight at the moment. That—my energy—seemed to vanish with Isis. "Okay," I stated. "I'll do it."

It was at that moment I heard a door close from down the hall. I looked up to see DJ slowly walk into the kitchen. His hair was disheveled and he hadn't shaved in a couple of days. He wore a ratty ripped tank top and jeans with holes in them. He dug his hands deep into his pockets. "Can I speak to Sam, Dad?" he muttered. I could see Jonathan choke back more tears. He looked at me, Jonathan did, from across the table. And something that was there, in his eyes, told me everything I needed to know about Isis's father. He would never not be tormented by this event.

"Absolutely," he said faking a smile and standing from the table. "I just have to make a run to town for a few things. The rest of the family will be here, soon. I want to make sure we have everything we need." He walked across the room and gave me an awkward, but tight hug. Despite my bitterness toward him, I hugged him. He exited the kitchen, and soon the house. Then, in the cold silence that I now felt like a permanent guest in the Cassidy house, DJ and I were left alone. I stood up from my seat at the table, and followed him as we made it back into the living room.

I tried not to look any further past DJ I didn't want to focus on Isis's bedroom door which could be seen at the start of the hallway. I dodged that side of the room and looked out the window instead. "I'm sorry I didn't answer when you knocked on my window," I said, half-heartedly. He didn't say anything but instead, just embraced me. His arms felt good around me, but I felt guilty inside—dirty. I was mad at so many people: Elliot, for inflicting such pain upon Isis. My parents and Jonathan for not taking the cries of little girls seriously enough. Mrs. Oates, who tried to listen too hard. Colin for no reason other than the fact he was an immature boy who couldn't possibly understand what was going on in our lives at the time. Guy for being Guy. And Cory, for failing to be the person that Isis expected him to be. And, truthfully, I was even mad at DJ for not being the kind of brother that notices right off the bat that something was wrong with his sister.

I sighed and pulled away from him. He could sense my distance—it didn't matter. He was just as disturbed as me. "I'm sorry," he finally said.

"What for?" I asked, softly. He shrugged his shoulders, but I knew there was something there, resting in all the corners of his mind. "

"Everything," he replied. I shook my head.

"You don't have any reason to apologize to me," I said quickly. The words tasted like betrayal coming out of my mouth. I didn't know why. "It's Elliot who should be apologizing. It's Elliot that should be paying for this crime," I said, harshly. DJ didn't say anything, he just looked out the window.

"Do you know where he went?" I asked. I felt my anger, my energy, spark a little within me. I wasn't sure why, but it was the most feeling I'd had since finding Isis. DJ shook his head.

"His house isn't finished—almost, maybe. Maybe he's staying there. I don't know," DJ said, without emotion. "It's not like we can do anything now," he said. I shivered at this response. I wanted to argue with him, but I couldn't, not now—not yet.

"I just wish…" I started. "I just wish we hadn't all failed her so miserably," I admitted. It was nothing to say to a man who was grieving his sister. Although, I was grieving a sister as well. I looked to him and I could see the tears begin to form in his eyes but he stopped them. He sniffed, as if it were his nose leaking instead, and cleared his throat. There were too many emotions running between the two of us. He reached for my hand, and I did not offer it, nor did I recoil at his touch.

It was then for some reason as I looked up at Isis's door and the hallway that followed, that something clicked within me. I almost couldn't breathe. I retracted my hand. I stopped, frozen, as if there were something within me—some force screaming at me that it was a lie. But it was too late to believe in fantasies of little girls. I had seen too much of what was behind the curtain now. My eyes traveled down the hall and I recalled the haunting words of a confessing Isis in the wood: He comes from down the hall.

I took a step back, looked at DJ and then I looked back at the hallway. I was losing my breath with every panicked second that this theory lingered inside my mind. Elliot's room was certainly in the hallway, but it was across from Isis' room. DJ was the one with the room down the hall. "Down the hall," I said, repeating my thoughts out loud.

"What?" DJ asked, looking to me curiously. I took another step backward. "What are you doing?" he asked—a worried tone lingered in his octave. I shook my head; my tears were abundant.

"Your room is down the hall," I said. He looked at me as if I had lost my mind. As if I were the sick one.

"What do you mean, Sam?" he asked, impatiently.

"She told me," my voice was weak and stuttering. "She told me…when she told me what was happening…she never said Elliot. I just…assumed. She said he comes down the hall and into her bedroom," I stated.

"Sam," DJ said, quickly and offensively. I took another step backward.

"I brought the police right to her but everyone was expecting her to point at Elliot," my voice was something of a cry. "And she didn't know how to tell anyone she'd been raped.

I mean, who could?" I nearly sounded hysterical. "But on top of having to admit that something so awful happened...HOW COULD SHE ADMIT TO ANYONE THAT IT WAS HER OWN MISERABLE BROTHER?" I screamed the words as loudly as I could as I backed away from the living room.

"Sam!" DJ yelled, but he offered no explanation—he offered no answers. I could see more emotion in him than before—he cried nearly as hard as me, but not quite. "Sam— you don't understand. Something...something has to be wrong with me," he pleaded. "It wasn't about having sex with her. It was..." his voice trailed off. He was admitting it now, and my stomach wanted to explode—I wanted to explode. My heart beat so loudly I could hear it pumping in my ears.

"It was about protecting her—at first. Everyone just went on and on about how beautiful she was and how much she looked like mom and guys said things about how much they wanted to pluck that cherry..." he heaved as he spoke. "I had to do something..." he said. I shook my head and turned around and walked quickly for the door. I winced, then screamed, as I heard his footsteps trample behind me. He grasped my wrist and turned me around, I could hear my wrist bones popping. "You can't say anything, Sam. Sam, you can't. I didn't mean to hurt her. I never wanted to hurt her. And I n- never wanted her to die!" His screams matched my own as I demanded him to let me go.

Quickly, I flung my foot upward, and fortunately for me, the tip of my sneaker slammed into his testicles. He whimpered and collapsed to the ground. Breathless, I tried to compose myself long enough to run out of the house. I ran as quickly as I could, across the Cassidy yard, and into my own. I panicked, knowing that if he could compose himself long enough to come after me, he would. And he would surely be able to outrun me. I fumbled with the doorknob, too scared to see how close he was behind me. As soon as I opened the door, I turned around and slammed it as hard and as quickly as I could. Though the glass window etched into our front door, I could see my clear path from the Cassidy house to mine. There was no sign of DJ.

I took a moment to try to steady my breath. I locked the door, failing the first time because of how badly my hands were shaking. Suddenly, I felt the grasp of a hand, a strong hand, on my shoulder. I screamed and flipped around, nearly bursting in tears. My father stood in front of me, in his regular ensemble, with a beer tucked firmly into his right hand. "What's wrong, Sam?" he said. It was the first sentence he'd spoken to me since the police wrongfully detained him.

I tried to speak, but it erupted into a manic cry. "Sam, slow down—talk to me," he said.

"He-he-he," I tried to catch my breath as I sobbed. "DJ just...he just....he hurt her, Dad!" It was him! He said it. It was him!" I cried. The look on my father's face was gentler than usual, and more than I ever expected. He had been quiet ever since he heard the news about Isis. It bothered him in a way he didn't expect, I think. "He-he-he hurt her!" I screamed. My father sat down the beer in his hand and put his hands on my shoulders.

"DJ did?" he asked, not in disbelief, but in shock.

"He hurt her!" I kept repeating. "He hurt her! I hurt her! I wasn't there! I didn't listen! I didn't see! I hurt her, Daddy. I killed her!" I screamed and when I did, I felt something inside me break—it wasn't just that I'd temporarily lost my voice, it was something else. Something I couldn't put my finger on. My father wrapped his arms around me and hugged me tightly. I couldn't remember the last time I was in my father's arms— and I couldn't think of any better place to be.

# Above The Pines

I stood in front of a mirror that hanged behind my bedroom door. Despite my appeal toward feminine wear, I scarcely recognized myself in a dress. That is what I was wearing, however, the morning of Isis's funeral. A black dress that reached my knees with thick black high heel shoes. In the time after my escape from the Cassidy house, my father had hardly left my side. It was both warranted and annoying. I dug out the dress from my grandmother's funeral two years prior. I barely fit into the dress anymore, but it would work.

I felt a nervous stabbing of pain in my stomach when I realized I would have to face not only a crowd, but DJ. I hadn't seen him since I kicked him and he hadn't bothered to come around. I knew he was waiting. He was waiting to see if I would call the police. He was waiting to see what I would do with the information he had given me. The truth was I hadn't done anything with that information. My grieving and sickness only doubled when I learned the truth. I had not only let the rapist go by unnoticed, just as everyone else had, I allowed myself to love him.

Now, every time the thought of his lips colliding into mine, the thoughts of us lying on his bed, kissing and holding each other, made me sick. I tried to distract myself from the thought, as today was a day to remember my friend. I clutched the poem tightly in my hand. Mr. Croft's assignment was to write a poem about how we find peace. I scanned over the lines and I almost smiled, realizing that all this time I thought I was the writer of the two of us, when in reality she was just as talented as myself. In fact, I thought of no better eulogy, than to let her words speak for themselves. I slid the poem back into a small pocket fashioned on my dress and sighed as I looked into the mirror one more time. I knew what Isis would say if she could see me now: Do you know how ridiculous you look? Even with those high heels, you're still the shortest girl in class.

My father was sober enough to drive to the church for the funeral. My mother claimed she was grieving too hard and couldn't possibly stand to see Isis laying in a casket. At least, that's the excuse she gave us this morning when my father tried to wake her up in time to get dressed. She'd been up pretty late the night before, drinking her sorrows away. I didn't mind, though. When my mother is sad, she talks. My father doesn't talk and neither do I. It's something we understand about one another, I suppose. We sat in silence on the way to the funeral and that was more than perfectly fine for me.

We reached Saint Marks Methodist Church. It was a beautiful church with a high steeple with a large bell located in the center. We arrived before mostly anyone else. I only recognized Jonathan's truck outside the church. My stomach twisted when I realized I would be in close proximity with him. "I can't go inside," I said as my father opened his door.

"Sam," he started, knowing where my mind was wandering. "You are safe. He's not going to hurt you here," he stated. I shook my head.

"It's not that, Dad," I started. "I just can't look at him." My dad shifted awkwardly in his seat, before opening his mouth to say something.

"Sam…we have to make it through this day for Isis.

Tomorrow, we can do something else. If you want to call the police, we can. If you want to talk to Jonathan, we can. Today, right now, you have to do this for her," he said. It was the most sensible I had ever heard my father speak—it was also the most sober.

Inside the church, I didn't see DJ, just Jonathan. He sat on the first pew of the sanctuary with the minister. I heard the minister's smooth voice say peaceful things as we approached. My dad stayed firmly by my side. As Jonathan noticed our arrival, he stood and greeted us, and took the time to introduce Pastor Gray. My father hugged Jonathan and I could hear crying come from them both. It was unusual for me to hear a grown man cry. In that moment I realized they were no more immortal than myself.

They walked to the back of the sanctuary, and before the minister joined them, he paused in front of me. "And you must be the brave one who is giving the eulogy today?" he said, as upbeat as one can while saying a sentence that contains the word eulogy. I nodded. "You must be a special girl," he said. I shook my head.

"No," I said, as I gestured toward the casket that sat open in front of the stage, which I had purposefully ignored thus far. "She was." The minister nodded solemnly and then motioned toward the casket. "Others will be arriving soon—if you want a few moments alone with her, I suggest you take them now," he said. I thanked him and he walked down the center aisle to join my father and Jonathan.

I took my time but eventually I approached the casket. I thought of all the things we'd done, and all the things we would've, but never had the chance to. I thought of the promises that were made and the ones that were broken. The all-nighters and the times we were fighting over something trivial and wouldn't speak for a week. I thought of chasing her throughout those miserable woods, hoping we wouldn't get anywhere near that pine tree she adored so much.

I reached her casket and looked downward. What I saw haunted me much more than I ever expected. The girl I saw in the casket wasn't Isis, but some cheap, shallow version of her that she always fought against. She was wearing make-up, not just the make-up applied to corpses to make them look less dead. No, she was wearing complete retail make-up. The kind one might wear on a fancy date. This was something I'd never seen on Isis's face before. She was wearing a dress and this too was something I'd never seen on Isis before. At least they got the color right: emerald. I stared for a long time not knowing what to say to her. I just kept staring at that make-up and that dress.

Finally and unexpectedly, I laughed. "And I thought I was the one that was going to look ridiculous," I said and laughed again. I'm sure, had anyone else heard me, my laughter, which echoed throughout the church, would have seemed morbid. And it's true: it felt a little morbid as it came out. I couldn't help but think about what Isis would say, if she were here. And I knew, without a doubt, she would be mortified to see herself looking such a way. I hated it for her—that her last appearance on this Earth would be looking a way she never looked whilst alive. I laughed, though, because I knew if she were standing beside me, looking at what I was looking at, she would be laughing, too—only harder.


I sat on the second row, with my father and some other strangers I thought might be some of the Cassidy family. They cried hard and some of them resembled Isis, or Jonathan, or DJ. Jonathan had invited me to sit on the front pew with him and DJ but I declined. I refused to look in DJ's general direction, and he refused to look up, period. I watched as other guests piled into the sanctuary. A line was formed at a side door that led them all to the casket to pay their final respects before taking a seat. I watched as Mrs. Oates entered, crying profusely. I could only imagine the guilt that resonated in her mind, now.

I watched as Cory entered. He looked scared, and pale. He

looked skinnier, too, oddly. He didn't have tears on his face, but he looked just as depressed as the rest of us. He lingered by her casket longer than most. And as he walked past me, to take his seat, I heard quiet sobs under his breath. I watched as Colin and Guy entered. I could see Guy's swollen jaw from where I was sitting. He looked ashamed, but not nearly enough.

Mr. Jacobsen, the bus driver, was next in line. He wore a plum suit with an old fedora tucked under his arm. It was the most dressed up I had ever seen him. The lines on his face spelt worry. I wondered what it was like, for a man in his golden years to peer down at a casket of a girl who had barely scratched the surface of adolescence. Mr. Croft was later in the line. He shook his head slightly as he got to Isis. It dawned on me that he was probably the only adult who really took us seriously. I would never forget him for that fact.


After a couple of songs and a few words by the minister, I was asked to come up to the stage. If it had been any other situation, I would surely be nervous. It wasn't the crowd of people that made me not want to approach the microphone, as I climbed the steps and stood at the podium. It wasn't even the fact that now DJ's attention would be directly focused on me. No, it was the fact that deep down, I wasn't ready to say goodbye to my best friend. I placed the folded piece of paper in front of me on the podium and slowly unfolded it. The creaking of the paper was absorbed in the microphone and echoed across the sanctuary.

I took a glance around the crowd and realized for the first time how many people showed up to pay their respects. The church was packed. People were having to stand along the sides of the walls. It seemed that the whole town was here to say goodbye and that infuriated me. It infuriated me because there were too many people here to let what happened to Isis, happen. There were too many people who would've helped her. And I knew that others could only do so much, that she would've had to do so much of it on her own but what could have been still bothered me.

I stood there in a room full of people I was positive didn't know the girl in the casket. I clutched her poem in my hand—her suicide note. Her last song. Her mention of peace. And I wondered if any of them deserved to hear it—even myself. And in that moment I honored Isis in the only way I knew how to—by not sharing words of her personality. By not sharing words written in her favorite emerald ink pen, but by being braver than I had ever been.

I folded the piece of paper back into the compact square in which it was first given to me. I took a deep breath, leaned forward into the microphone and uttered the only sentence that I felt needed to be uttered: "DJ did it." I proceeded to walk away from the podium. The murmurs started at once and they didn't bother to be subtle as I stepped off the stage. There were several shocked faces, but I didn't make eye contact with any of them as I walked past the pews, for the side door.

DJ looked at me. I could feel his eyes—he wasn't angry, not at me anyway. He was something else. A feeling or an emotion I'm sure that I've never felt. I did, unfortunately, catch a glimpse of Jonathan. His eyes were frightened—there was a hollow look about him. The kind of look one would have after being shot in the chest. I imagine that's the only comparable feeling, when you realize you haven't lost one child, but two.

I exited the side door of the church and onto the sidewalk that ran parallel with the main road. I walked past the town square, and past the school. I followed that road to my neighborhood, and then I cut down my street. I walked past my house, and the Cassidy house, and right through our back yards, too. It wasn't until I reached the tree line that I began to slow down.

A lot of things changed in that town. Mr. Croft and Mrs. Oates, along with the rest of the school staff and student body, raised enough money to start a foundation for abused women and children in Isis's name. Carly confessed a few weeks later than she had been sexually abused and once she named her attacker, ten other women came forward to confess the same thing. Guy never really changed that much, but he stopped being such a bully. I'm not sure what happened to Colin, but he moved away after he graduated. I heard a rumor a while back that he married and had a child. I hope he's happy.

Cory became a minister and his church specialized in providing shelter, care, and protection for anyone being sexually and physically abused. I've been to a few of his services—they're nice. I found Elliot and apologized. He accepted graciously. He still lives in the house he built. DJ broke down and confessed after the funeral. He went to prison for five years for the crime. The last thing I heard about him was that he was a drug addict, bouncing back and forth between prisons. Jonathan disowned his son, sold the house, and moved away. I haven't spoken to him in years. I wouldn't even know what to say now.

My father and I became close after the funeral. We developed the relationship we had both always wanted. He cleaned up his act, and stayed sober. My mother did not, we buried her ten years later—we held her funeral in the same church.

As I walked through the woods, I thought about how quickly and elegantly Isis would move past these branches. I did not. I finally made it, however, to the pine—Isis's favorite. I stared at the monster before me. I could finally see why Isis loved it so much. It stood tall and strong among the rest. It was a pine unlike any other surrounding it. Its presence alone should make the other pines be happy they were pines, as well. It marveled in its roots, faced the sun, and welcomed the wind to flow gently between its branches.

And in that thought, I realized that Isis was like that pine tree. She was the pine in which we all gazed upon. She was the pine that inspired all of us to beat onward. I slipped off my shoes, looked up, took a deep breath and reached out for the branch closest to me. I pulled myself up, and slowly, I began to climb the pine by myself. As I worked my way up the branches, occasionally slipping, I thought about every time before, when I climbed it. I thought about how I complained. I thought about how I nearly killed myself from the climb had it not been for Isis who always caught me.

She wasn't there to catch me this time, but I knew that in some way, she was there, helping me grasp another branch. It was then, in that climb, that I thought about her poem. The poem that resided in my dress pocket. The poem in her emerald ink handwriting. The poem of her place of peace: "Above the Pines."

*Above the Pines*
*In the sky*
*The beloved timberline*
*Hear the white heron cry*

*From the depths of the wood*
*In the center of my mind*
*Like no one else could*
*I'm at ease with my timberline.*

I finally reached the branch where I always stopped. It sat two below the top, just under the top of the tree. I heaved another breath and climbed two more branches, reaching the top of the tree. A broken finger nail, and a ripped dress later, I was sitting atop the pine tree, gazing at the timberline around me. I took in the skyline from the city, off in the distance, as did I take in the mountains.

Isis was right about me. I did get out of that town. I did make it to the city and earlier than I expected to do so, just like Isis said I would. I applied for a program that allowed me to finish obtaining my high school degree whilst taking college courses at a local university in the city. Because of the program, I was able to graduate college nearly two years earlier than the rest of my peers.

I landed a job right after that and I've been a working writer in the city ever since. I don't know if Isis really could see the future or not, when she dreamt, but I know she was right about me. Maybe she just believed in me like when I would climb the pine, even when I didn't believe in myself. She never said she would make it to the mountains, but that she would make it someplace nice. I looked to the sky as I grasped firmly onto the branches just below me. I saw the clouds part and I felt the sun hit my face. There was something about the clarity of that timberline air that put me in the peace Isis felt. I believed in that moment that she was in a better place.

I never made it back out to the pines after that day. A few years later the entire wood was torn down to make way for a new subdivision. A subdivision of small, flat houses. Houses that didn't come close to the timberline. Houses that couldn't see the city.

*End.*

www.ingramcontent.com/pod-product-compliance
Lightning Source LLC
Chambersburg PA
CBHW071133200626
46817CB00018B/2929